CRACKS IN THE COBBLESTONE

CRACKS IN THE COBBLESTONE

BY
SUSAN E. SAGARRA

Doug,

we might not solve all of life's mysteries but we can enjoy the journey!! :)

Susan E. Sagarra

Oak Tree Press  Hanford, CA

Oak Tree Press
Publishers Since 1998

For information, address Oak Tree Press, 1820 W. Lacey Boulevard, Suite 220, Hanford, CA 93230.

Oak Tree Press books may be purchased for educational, business, or sales promotional purposes. Contact Publisher for quantity discounts.

First Edition, March 2015

ISBN 978-1-61009-168-8
LCCN 2015931998

In loving memory of my parents, Ron and Earlyne Sagarra, who never told their story about life and love, they lived it.

APRIL 12

Meghan Murphy's heels clicked on the cobblestones as she walked along Main Street.

The clickety-clack echoed annoyingly between the decaying buildings lining the street. Still, some men's gazes lingered a little longer once they spotted the confident strides of the legs attached to those metallic sounds.

Meghan's right heel caught in the crack between the cobblestones and she nearly walked right out of her red pumps. She didn't dare view the onlookers as she recovered and opened the door to the dark shadows of the smoky yet not smoke-filled Mug's Pub. A gust of wind temporarily swept up her straight, long brunette hair as she took refuge inside.

She took a moment to let her eyes adjust from the brightness outside to the darkness within, then chose an empty bar stool as far away from the front door as possible. She had one eye set on the front door but also kept tabs behind her, as reflected in the mirror hanging on the opposite side of the once-pristine wood bar.

After she pulled out a dainty cigar, the bartender clipped the end and lit it for her. Then she casually ordered a Miller Light and a shot of whiskey. She did not care for whiskey but family tradition called for her to drink it to alleviate her sore throat.

While she pondered her drinks and took a drag on her cigar, she marveled at the vintage collectibles in the place. She discovered something new during each visit. Dark wooden shelves hung just out of reach of patrons on each of the interior walls. Each shelf was adorned with a hodgepodge of colorful collectible items. The place was a mini museum of old dolls, toys, rusted metal signs including a faded stop sign, old-fashioned toy fire trucks, old-time bar fixture lights, and black and white photographs of yesteryear.

One of her favorites was the Pabst Blue Ribbon chalkboard sign with the words "Free Beer Tomorrow" scrawled in white chalk. Silly bar humor.

White Christmas lights were strung along some of the shelves while colored lights framed others. The lights were displayed in as much of a hodgepodge fashion as the collection. Their purpose was to decorate, not illuminate.

Meghan took full advantage of her brief respite from the outside world. Mug's Pub was her favorite escape, where she wouldn't be bothered with real-life problems, and could contemplate. Today, she found herself pondering her newest dilemma; the investigation that she had to pretend didn't exist. It was the weekend; that official business could be saved for the work week, she told herself. Then she laughed.

"Since when have I ever shut off 'official business,' weekend or not?" the work-a-holic said to no one in particular.

***

Harrison Parker's right heel clicked on the cobblestones, reminding him to find a shoe cobbler. No need to announce his presence everywhere.

He strode into Mug's Pub. Turning to his immediate right, he chose the seat at the end of the L-shaped marble-covered and freshly-shined wood bar. He sat with his back to the cold, brick wall. He kept an eye on the front door while searching the length of the restaurant on the opposite side. Harrison Parker was always on alert, but more likely just slightly paranoid.

A gritty-looking couple sat in the middle booth of the three that were situated to the left, deeper into the restaurant. A few stragglers sat along the length of the bar, each drinking alone but feeling the comfort of someone nearby. Several empty tables—some short, some high—were arranged in total disarray, it seemed, down the middle of the place. It created the effect of almost separating the bar from the three booths, although the tables seemed to favor the booths.

He noted that straddling each side of the front door were two sunrooms with bay windows. Each mini dining room had a table for four and curtains that were pulled open on each side. He wondered if anyone ever unhitched the curtains for privacy. Curiously, the side facing the street had floor-to-ceiling windows with no such adornment, much like a street display in one of those fancy clothing stores he had seen in the big city.

Harrison pondered the intriguing arrangement of collectibles and lights lining the shelves around the room.

A man played the piano, which was on a tiny stage in the back of the bar. Harrison pulled out his crumpled pack of cigarettes, dislodged one and took a deep puff. The bartender came over to the sharp-dressed man, who would only be a stranger until he introduced himself.

"Welcome to Mug's Pub. I'm Frank Henderson. But please, just call me Frank. What brings you to our fine town on this pleasant day?" said the proprietor, with a sincere smile in his eyes.

"Gin and tonic, please," Harrison replied. "Does your piano player take any requests?"

Frank had seen this type before, with salt-and-pepper unkempt hair and a brooding, mysterious persona. Frank poured the drink and handed it to the fella. Harrison grabbed the drink and tipped his head in gratitude before taking a heavy sip.

"Robert Woodson's his name, the piano player," Frank said. "He pretty much does whatever he wants, when he wants. He's a friendly guy but don't interrupt him when he's creating. He doesn't like to be disturbed. Interrupt his train of thought and he gets sidetracked. He sure can play that piano, though, I tell 'ya. I've never seen anyone tickle the ivories the way he can. And it seems so effortless. Whereabouts you from? Them are some spiffy clothes you're wearin'. We like our folks to loosen up, sit back and relax in here. So feel free to enjoy yourself."

Harrison took another sip of his drink.

"Appreciate the heavy hand on the drink, Frank," Harrison said dismissively but still sounding polite. He even managed a slight smile.

Frank chuckled to himself and went back to tending to the other customers, who had witnessed the exchange with piqued ears and side glances but never looked directly at the stranger.

Harrison noticed a young, attractive woman seemingly sitting by herself at the opposite end of the bar, slowly sipping her beverage. He could see she was a lady, with her white-gloved hand, a bonnet adorned with purple ribbons and matching parasol occupying the spot next to her.

She appeared lost in deep thought, nearly oblivious to anything else going on around her. Her ocean blue eyes only lit up when Frank approached. They seemed comfortable with each other. The woman seemed familiar to Harrison, although he did not know her. Normally, he would have thought it odd for a lady of her seeming outward social stature to be sitting in a place like this by herself. But he had recently learned that nothing about life was normal.

LATER THAT DAY

Meghan left Mug's Pub after an hour. She walked across the cobblestone street, and nearly caught her heel again. She just kept walking.

She listened to the odd mix of horses' hooves, carriage wheels and the horsepower of the modern vehicles. She enjoyed the different periods of time clashing. The horse-drawn carriages in particular reminded her that there still was some quaint, small town atmosphere in this hectic world.

She walked north a block to the last building at the end of the street - 340 N. Main Street. Her home away from home.

It was a nice, sunny spring day but she reminded herself that she should try to do some writing. She also needed to read the newspapers that were stacking up. But she decided to save that for later in the week.

When she walked into the foyer of the old building, she took a quick look at the awards, honors and official resolutions that paid homage to those who came before her. This was her ritual each time she entered the building, using it as her own form of motivation and inspiration, to aspire to become as great as those honored in the display case. She lingered a little longer today because nobody was around to watch. Then she turned and walked noisily up the linoleum steps, with her heels announcing her entrance to no one.

After spending some time inside the cramped, dank building, she realized her mind really would like to stretch itself outside. She headed out the back of the building and went across the street to the park that ran adjacent to the lazy river.

***

Harrison left the pub after five of Frank's special drinks and one of the most delicious meals he had ever experienced: a hefty portion of rare prime rib, au gratin potatoes and a generous salad.

The most Frank could get out of the stranger was that his name was Harrison. Although he was not afraid of the stranger, Frank had the feeling that no one welcomed the opportunity to be on the wrong end of one of his bad moods.

As the pleasant spring day turned into an even more pleasant spring night, Harrison strolled north to The Brass Inn, located at the northernmost point of Main Street. A beautiful young lady, whom he had seen talking briefly to the attractive white-gloved woman seated by herself at the bar earlier, approached the door of the elegant hotel at the same time. Harrison opened the door, tipped his hat and silently motioned for her to enter. The woman paid no heed and did not even thank him.

Harrison entered the newly refurbished lobby and admired again how exquisite it was. The desk clerk had told him that a cyclone destroyed much of the north side of the 3-story building a decade ago but that it turned out to be the best thing that happened to the place. It was rebuilt better than ever. In Harrison's opinion, it was spectacular, although a bit out of place compared to some of the other buildings he had been in and out of along the street.

After a moment's pause, Harrison walked silently up the staircase, except for the occasional creaking of the wood hidden underneath the plush red velvet carpet. It was a nice change from the symphony outside: the clappity-clop of the horse-drawn carriages and the loud vehicle engines, accompanied with his heel clanking on the brick street. His hand lingered along the intriguing red, soft, velvet-lined hand rail.

Once he arrived at the second floor, Harrison headed to his room – 212 – which would serve as his home for at least the next couple of weeks. He had chosen a room that faced the front of the building, overlooking Main Street. The desk clerk had suggested the quieter rooms in the back, overlooking the park and river. But Harrison knew it was ideal viewing things from the best vantage point and he knew that the front of the building would offer a nice snippet of Main Street and all that inhabited it.

SATURDAY, APRIL 13

The sound of birds chirping, horse hooves and carriage wheels clopping along the cobblestones stirred Harrison from his slumber. It was a mellower sound than the evening provided. The sun was shining brightly through the thin yellow curtains that adorned the bedroom window.

He didn't know what Frank put in those drinks, or perhaps there was a secret ingredient in the prime rib, but he had slept deeper than he had in months. It also might have been the change of scenery, after all that he had been through over the past year.

He shaved, showered and dressed, then walked back down the block to have breakfast at Mug's Pub. Apparently, everyone else in this quaint town with the quirky name–Tirtmansic—had the same idea. As he opened the door, the chatter, laughter and sounds from a fiddle in the distance smacked full force into his slightly hung over head. The place was packed with men, women and children. The pub had become a diner overnight, although the darkness prevailed.

Harrison couldn't get a seat with his back to the wall but he did manage to squeeze into a spot at the bar between two other men who were quietly drinking their coffee. The mirror sat opposite him so he had a limited view of what lurked behind him.

Frank spotted him and smiled knowingly.

"Good day, sir. How did you sleep over there at The Brass Inn? It's quite a majestic place inside, isn't it?" Frank asked. "Can I get you a cup of coffee?"

Harrison nodded yes and as Frank poured the smooth, steaming black brew into the cup sitting on the bar in front of him, he asked, "Cream? Sugar? Irish cream?"

"Just straight black, thank you, Frank," Harrison said, not needing a refresher course on the alcohol just yet. "Do you have a breakfast menu?"

Frank searched the backsplash of the bar for a long moment and finally produced a couple of stained copies.

"Here 'ya go. They might be outdated. I'll be back to get your order after you've had a chance to study it," Frank said with a chuckle, walking away shaking his head.

The man to Harrison's right said, "The eggs Benedict are the best within 100 miles, although you can't go wrong with any of the food here. The cook, Frank's wife Lila, is amazing with everything she creates in her little kitchen tucked away in the back."

Harrison nodded acknowledgement to the gentleman, figuring he must be an authority on the matter, and set the menu aside.

Frank returned and asked, "What'll it be, chap?"

"I'll have the eggs Benedict," he said.

"Excellent choice. Comes with hash browns and toast. Fill 'er up?" Frank asked, with the silver server already tipped and coffee flowing into Harrison's cup. Harrison nodded yes and said "Thanks."

"So this is the place to be on Saturday mornings, eh?" Harrison asked the man to his right, in an attempt to beat the man to idle chit-chat and start asking him the questions. Always the interviewer, never the interviewee.

"This place and there's a great breakfast place down on South Main Street," the man said. "It's bigger than here so it can hold more people. But the people here are friendlier and more sincere. You can come and be yourself here and nobody messes with you. It's also easier to find out the truth of what's going on around town instead of all the gossip. Name's Robert. Glad you came back."

"Name's Harrison. Where'd you learn to play the piano like that?" Harrison asked.

"Basically taught myself, just fiddlin' around," Robert said. "My parents never had enough money to get me lessons but we had a piano that just sat in our living room collecting dust. Was my grandmother's and nobody ever played it. When I was bored on rainy and snowy days, I would just sit and mess around. I'm not really that talented. Just know enough to entertain the folks. Taught myself enough songs to keep it going all evening."

"I never could play anything. I admire anyone who can play a musical instrument," Harrison said, keeping the focus on Robert.

"I officially play here every night except Mondays and Tuesdays. Others join in sometimes. But you'll almost always find someone playing some kind of music in here," Robert said, nodding toward the fiddler on the stage, who was managing to complement the laughter and chatter with his own melody. "We have some dancing girls who like to come in and get the crowd riled up. They're a fun group, lots of laughter and just pure joy to play music while they are dancing and having a good time. Sometimes we have comedians who take the stage. Occasionally I try to be the comedian but I'm not real good at it."

He laughed at himself.

A young man who looked like an offspring of Frank's arrived with Harrison's breakfast, which looked like it could feed two adults and one child.

"You were right about the eggs Benedict," Harrison said to Robert, as he wolfed it down.

After another cup of coffee, Harrison paid his bill, shook Robert's hand and thanked him for the culinary advice.

"Be sure to come back later for more piano, and the Saturday night frivolity. Never know what you might come across in here," Robert said with a sly grin and a wink.

"Will do," Harrison said and left. The place seemed to have become even more crowded in the time that he had eaten his breakfast.

As he stepped back into the sunshine, Harrison scanned the street for a taxi. He spotted a sleek, newer model black Cadillac and hailed it. Climbing in, he asked to be driven to Annabelle Adams' School for Young Ladies, on the other side of town.

The driver slightly raised his eyebrow.

"Interested in checking out the place for your, uh, daughter?" the driver asked.

After all, this guy was alone and had just walked out of a pub at 9 a.m. And now he was headed to a school for young ladies.

Harrison simply said, "Something like that."

The driver proceeded to tell him about the school, particularly the history of the family and the grounds before it became a school. Harrison pretended not to listen.

As the driver pulled up to the entrance, Harrison saw the beauty for himself. They drove under one side of a two-sided white stone arch entranceway and up a narrow tree-lined path. The treetops seemed to hover as high as the clouds in the sky.

The place exuded peacefulness, something sorely lacking in Harrison's own life.

Some young ladies sat at picnic tables quietly studying and others rocked in four-seat wood swings, talking and laughing as if life only existed for those two reasons. Harrison asked the driver to drop him off at the end of the path, where another path cut across to create a T-shaped intersection. He paid the driver for a round-trip, asking if he could return in an hour.

The campus held three stately buildings: one indicated it was the ladies' dormitory, one indicated it was classrooms and the far one on the right indicated that it was an administrative building. In the distance behind the ladies' dormitory he could see a couple of small houses. A gazebo commanded attention in the middle of campus, standing by itself on the massive lush green lawn. The rare slice of sun cutting through the trees seemed to shine a spotlight upon it.

He walked up the stone steps of the administrative building, his heel clicking all the way.

He struggled to open the 4-inch thick solid wood doors and found himself inside an alcove with a similar arch entranceway, on a smaller scale than the one that greeted him on the drive in. He closed the door, interrupting the silence inside, and started wandering down the sparkling clean marble-floored hallway, finding mostly closed doors and empty offices.

But he knew that the president of the school would be there. He knew that the man worked on Saturdays while his wife went to tea and the shoppes on Main Street with her lady friends. She sometimes took the teachers and her students with her as well, just for a special treat.

When he arrived at the end of the hallway, a round, tall man stood expectantly, staring at him over a pair of wire-rimmed glasses. He not only had heard the wood door closing upon Harrison's entrance but also heard each click of the nail in Harrison's shoe.

"Greetings, Mr. Thornton, Harrison's the name, pleased to meet you," Harrison said, as he offered his hand for a shake, purposely failing to mention his last name. He already knew that this man was a sly one and didn't know how powerful his resources were. He didn't want to take any chances on him finding out who he was and what he was up to, at least not yet.

"Mr. Harrison, how can I help you?" James Thornton said, in an arrogant tone.

Harrison couldn't help but notice the shine from Thornton's mostly bald head. Two patches of graying hair somehow had been spared on each side above his ears.

"I wanted to inquire about schooling for my daughter next fall," Harrison said. "You see, my wife, who was a teacher, recently died and I have a 6-year-old daughter and well, I'm sure you understand. It's difficult being a single father and trying to work and educate her properly. I have heard about your school's excellent reputation."

Thornton stared at his visitor. Every stranger was a potential threat in Thornton's mind, and someone who intruded on his Saturdays–let alone knew he was there on a Saturday–put Thornton on guard. Harrison would become one more person for Thornton to scrutinize, and destroy if needed. Or potentially bribe. Thornton prided himself on the fact that he had learned long ago to size up the competition and determine other people's weaknesses immediately. He may or may not need to use the information against that person but it was helpful to have it at his disposal. It was even more valuable when he needed to coerce someone into being an ally.

"Well, Mr. Harrison, why don't you come on in and have a seat and we can discuss this further," Thornton said, raising an eyebrow and smirking as he turned away from Harrison. "You know, we have a shoe cobbler in town."

Harrison ignored the jab.

"Please, have a seat," Thornton motioned to the stiff-backed chair on one side of the desk while Thornton ensconced himself in his plush executive chair. "As you said, Annabelle Adams' School for Young Ladies is a fine institution. We accept young ladies from highly sophisticated backgrounds and offer an excellent education to young ladies who have a tremendous amount of talent, potential...and of course, social stature."

Thornton let the insinuation sit for a moment, noting that Harrison's clothes seemingly were bought off the rack and not exactly starched to perfection. The condition of the man's shoes also indicated a lack of funds. Harrison laughed to himself about people's perceptions. Frank had sized him up to be a sharp-dressed man; Thornton looked down his bespectacled nose at him.

"Money is not an issue, Mr. Thornton," Harrison said. "I can assure you that I can provide everything that my daughter needs and wants, and then some. I just cannot provide her with the 'excellent education,' as you put it, with my current situation and where we live now. I believe she has the potential that you indicate."

"Well, we shall have to put her, uh, what did you say your daughter's name is?" Thornton asked.

"I didn't. But it's Penelope," Harrison replied.

"Ah, yes, well we will need to meet the young Penelope in person and put her through rigorous reading, writing and arithmetic testing to see if she is suited for placement here," Thornton said. "I also will have to personally view your financial portfolio. It's just a formality, I can assure you. We must do a thorough check of all our potential students and their parents' ability to fund a proper education. But as you likely are aware, nobody is here today to handle the details and I gather you did not come prepared to hand over your financial details just yet. So how about you return on Monday with your lovely daughter and I can have my wife take both of you on a tour of the campus and set her down for the testing? Please bring your financial statements as well, but we must be discreet so make sure you deliver those to me or my secretary, Ruth, personally. There is no need to involve my wife in those particular details."

Thornton signaled that the meeting was finished by standing up and coming from behind his desk to shake Harrison's hand. Harrison took one last glance around the office, smiled at the robust president and shook the man's hand.

"I will be back," Harrison said, not committing to a specific date. "Thank you for your time today."

Thornton walked Harrison all the way to the heavy wooden doors, not even bothering to share any of the stories of the portraits or paintings adorning the walls along the hallway, or give any type of history of the school. Thornton already had his mind made up that Mr. Harrison's young daughter would not, in fact, be attending school here so no need to waste time explaining anything to this poor chap. Besides, this bloke had interrupted a pressing matter that required Thornton's full attention and that annoyed him even more.

"Good day, Mr. Harrison," Thornton said with a fake smile as he shut the heavy door behind Harrison. Harrison heard the clicking of the lock.

Harrison had made initial contact; that was all he needed for now. While waiting for his driver to return, Harrison perused the grounds. He was surprised that the president had not walked him all the way to the entrance, although he was quite certain that Mr. Thornton was watching from his barricaded perch.

Harrison paused to take in the solitude of the tree-filled grounds and smiled to himself, actually thinking about what a great place this really would be for Penelope, to have some much-needed youthful interaction and distraction from her brooding father.

The buildings were large and stately, with massive white columns holding up the front entrances with perched porches that held fancy, lady-like furniture for lounging. He could imagine Penelope running through the grass and lazily reading underneath the welcoming trees that intermittently let in the shade and sun as they swayed in the breeze. She needed some of that restfulness in her life. Harrison's current mental state and moodiness were not helping her.

Harrison met the driver at the entrance and the driver asked if he would like to return to Mug's Pub. Harrison asked him if he could just give him a driving tour of the little town. The driver pointed out landmarks, the good places to eat, the bad places to eat, hear music, find female companionship, shoot pool or just go to quietly read or study. The driver also gave Harrison a history lesson about the town and even some of the kinfolk.

When they had returned to The Brass Inn, Harrison asked how he might get a hold of the driver in the future and the man jotted down a phone number. He told him to ring him up anytime, although he had Sundays off. Harrison paid a little extra for the tour and thanked him for the information.

He walked into the stunning hotel and walked up the velvet-lined stairs to his room. He intended to take a nap but wrote down some notes first. He finally did lay down for about 30 minutes, but was restless so he took a walk down to the other end of Main Street.

He found a shoe cobbler but it had a "closed" sign hanging on the inside of the glass door. He strolled into an ice creamery and purchased a hefty chocolate ice cream cone, finally realizing he had not eaten lunch. He savored the treat while sitting out in front on one of the benches, watching the cars and horse-drawn carriages and all the people going to and fro. They seemed to be oblivious to the new guy in town, although he knew that in any small town, everyone knew everyone and knew when a stranger was in their presence. Few would make direct eye contact with him but they knew he was there.

He sat there for a couple of hours just taking it all in and marveled at the fact that not one person approached him. He attributed it to his pervasive dark mood that seemed to create a shelter around him.

When it was dinnertime, he walked into a small restaurant on the south end of Tirtmansic. It really was a winery and because it had outdoor dining, he requested a table under the trees. The place was far from crowded. He ate a hearty meal of steak and potatoes. Not normally a wine drinker, preferring the heavy liquor, the waitress convinced him that a fine red wine would in fact go well with his steak.

When he finished his meal in quiet solitude, he noticed that the other tables had filled up so he slipped out onto the sidewalk to enjoy the evening. The breeze had picked up a bit in the descending darkness. He walked back up to his hotel but on the way, heard laughter, music and frivolity emanating from Mug's Pub so went back to what quickly was becoming his favorite hangout.

The pub was packed beyond capacity, mostly with men but also several women who dared to go into such a raucous place on a Saturday night. Cigar smoke and cigarette smoke mingled but it was so dark, one could not see the haze, only feel it. Harrison walked over to the spot where he originally had plunked himself the previous night and stood, leaning his tired body against the wall.

He asked the bartender for a beer. From across the bar, Robert Woodson caught his eye and smiled appreciatively as he teased the piano keys. Harrison nodded in acknowledgement.

Harrison noticed that President Thornton was sitting in the farthest booth in the back, entertaining three ladies—none of whom, Harrison deduced, were his wife—and one other gentleman. They all appeared to have imbibed quite a bit and were yakking and laughing so hard that it almost drowned out the piano music.

Harrison stayed hidden in the shadows, trying to blend into the wall.

On a break, the piano player came over to Harrison and handed him another beer.

"Quite a different atmosphere from earlier, isn't it?" Woodson said. "Saturday nights usually get a little crazy, when the men come in and hide away from their wives and the women who don't act like ladies come out to play."

Harrison nodded his gratitude for the beer and acknowledgement of what Robert said. But he really did not feel like idle chit-chat and hoped that the man's break would be short-lived. He liked the sound of his fingers on the piano keys more than his chatter right now.

Soon after that thought, a young red-headed girl sidled up to Woodson and said "Hey, honey, you gonna play my song for me tonight?"

"Of course, darling," Woodson said with a wink and a grin toward Harrison. "You know I always save that song just for you on Saturday nights. I'll play it in my next set. But you have to pay attention for the whole set because I can't tell 'ya when I might throw it in there."

"I always pay attention to you, Woodsy boy," the red-head said with a girlish giggle. "Now, who is this fine specimen of a man you're talkin' to and why haven't you introduced me yet?"

Her eyes seductively focused on the new man.

"His name's Harrison, just got into town," Robert said. "He don't speak too much but I have a feeling we'll learn more about him when he loosens up and gets to know us. Harrison, this is Miss Misty. She's a bright and talented young lady."

"Pleased to meet you," Harrison said with a smirk.

"Pleasure to meet *you,* Mr. Harrison," Miss Misty said with a wink and a broad smile. "I hope you'll stick around 'cause we definitely could use some new, mighty fine men around here to shake things up a bit, if 'ya know what I mean? Present company excepted, of course, everyone loves Woodsy here," as she gave Robert a friendly pinch on the arm.

"Well, I gotta go see to my friends but I'll be back to check on both of you later, darlin's," Misty said as she sauntered off with another wink and smile for both men.

Robert then said to Harrison, "So I heard you're checkin' out Annabelle Adams' School for Young Ladies. How old is your daughter, or do you have more than one?"

Word travels fast, Harrison thought to himself.

"She's 6," Harrison said, thinking the piano man probably already knew that, too.

"Mighty fine school they have there. Lots of money floating around," Robert said, telling Harrison something that he in fact already knew. "I'm tellin' 'ya, too much money floatin' around there, if you catch my drift."

Harrison caught more than Robert's drift. He already knew there was more money "floating around," or rather, floating out of, the place than just what it took in from the annual room, board and tuition for the relatively small number of young ladies who attended the school.

"What do you know about that situation?" Harrison asked, his interest piqued somewhat.

"We should talk sometime soon," Robert said, leaning in and lowering his voice. "But not right now."

Then Robert said it was time for him to return to "ticklin' the ivories." Robert seemed to play for two hours straight without a break, and after three more beers and two gin and tonics, Harrison called it quits.

There would be plenty of time to have a real conversation with Robert some other time, perhaps in a much quieter setting.

APRIL 14

Each time Meghan started an investigation, she was prepared for it to be a long, drawn out ordeal. Part of it was her own fault, as she wanted to make sure she covered absolutely every angle and every aspect before she even tried to sit down and write about it. She immersed herself in her subject because it was the only way to really tell the story. She knew that her writing was only as good as the subject involved. And the more passionate her sources were about the topic, the better the story.

But it all required time to develop. Her editor did not like the slow pace but was always extremely satisfied with the end result, and ultimately, the reaction from the newspaper's readers. So he put up with it—and Meghan—more than he desired.

Meghan was just starting her investigation of the nursing home located on the other side of town. She had to be cautious because the nursing home advertised—a lot—in *The Main Informer*. Meghan knew the score on that. Nonetheless, the place needed to be investigated, for the sake of the residents, the employees, and the taxpayers.

She had been vague when her editor asked her what she was investigating this time. In actuality, she never revealed her hand until she knew what she was looking for and knew for certain what she had found. It was a silly little game they played.

On more than one occasion, her investigations had been quashed before they barely got started because of somebody's connection at the newspaper to the subject, particularly a financial connection. It was the curse of living in as small a town as Tirtmansic. In reality, it was a curse for all journalists. There was a dangerous trend toward catering to paying customers frequently trumping thorough, investigative reporting.

It was just starting to affect Meghan and her colleagues, although such financial and political influence no doubt had been going on for years. Economic realities dictated that advertisers had more influence than good, sound, watchdog journalism.

Still, Meghan stood up every chance she got for her readers, the taxpayers and voters of Tirtmansic. She considered it her duty to report about fraudulent practices, excessive government spending and illegal activities. The publisher and editor both claimed to like the controversy that her reporting inevitably created, but they also feared the controversy. Sometimes that fear drove their decisions in the wrong direction.

Undeterred, Meghan made a list of potential sources to contact and started formulating her list of questions. She also needed to search old newspapers to see what she could find out about the property and former inhabitants.

Because it was a nice day and Meghan was not on deadline, she walked south three blocks to make some requests at the town's historical society. They had archives of every newspaper that ever existed locally but also had some of the more prominent national and international publications available for viewing.

Her friend at the historical society, Diane, greeted her with a smile and said, "Good morning, Meghan. Always a pleasure to see you. What can I help you find today?"

Meghan said she needed every article she could find regarding the Mercy Angels Nursing Home. She also wanted land plot documents indicating everyone who had ever owned the land and developed previously on it.

"Oh, and please keep it quiet that I inquired," Meghan said. "I need this to be done without anyone knowing."

Diane winked and said, "Of course, Meghan. We're just like reporters, we never reveal anything to anyone."

Diane told Meghan to come back the next morning and peruse through what her staff could pull from their files. Meghan thanked her and went in search of something much more desirable—lunch.

She walked further south to the old-fashioned ice creamery, where she could enjoy a light chicken salad sandwich on a croissant and a decadent double-fudge brownie ice cream delight.

After going for a leisurely stroll to the end of Main Street, to walk off the ice cream she told herself, Meghan headed back to *The Main Informer*. As she passed by one of her favorite haunts, Mug's Pub, she heard music coming from within. She thought that was strange, as Mug's Pub was only open in the middle of the day on Fridays and Saturdays these days.

But she clearly heard someone playing the piano and it was coming from inside the pub. She tried the doors but they were sealed shut. She peeked into the front windows to see if she could view anyone sitting at the piano in the back of the building. But the dark wood interior combined with the lack of lighting made it difficult for her to see much past the first stool at the bar.

She enjoyed the tunes for a moment and then chalked it up to the fact that maybe the piano player was just practicing for his Friday night gig and she just could not see that far in the darkness. She walked back up the street to finish out her afternoon by making some phone calls.

But the thought that someone was playing the piano in the middle of the day lingered in her mind all afternoon. She knew the piano player. He didn't need to practice. He knew all the songs inside and out; she bet he would find a way to play them backwards if someone made the request.

When she was done working for the day, she talked a new business associate she had met at a Chamber of Commerce meeting, Rebecca, into meeting at the pub for a cocktail before heading home. When they walked in, it was apparent that several others had the same idea. They couldn't find two spots at the bar but found an empty booth in the far corner.

When the waitress came over to take their order, Meghan asked her if someone had been playing piano during the day. The waitress laughed and said, "That's highly doubtful, honey. I was the first one to get here today and the locks had been changed for some reason so I had to wait for the owner to arrive. Plus, Jonathan's the only one who knows how to play the piano around here and he's out of town until Friday. What can I get the two of you?"

After the waitress walked away, Rebecca asked, "What was that about?"

"I was walking past here after lunch this afternoon and heard someone playing the piano," Meghan said. "But the front door was locked and it was pitch black in here. I couldn't see anyone in here and there weren't any lights on. But I know I heard the piano, this piano, being played."

"Are you sure it wasn't coming from another building?" Rebecca asked. "You know how things echo because of the close proximity of these old buildings."

Meghan shook her head.

"No, it clearly was from within here and it was Jonathan's style of playing. Maybe I'm just losing my mind. Other weird things have been going on lately."

"Like what?"

The waitress arrived with their cocktails and Meghan said "Never mind. It's just my imagination running wild. To no more work for the day! Cheers!"

Rebecca was not going to let it go.

"Tell me what's going on, Meghan."

Meghan sighed, fearing she would chase off her new friend before they had a chance to learn each other's quirks.

She finally leaned into the table and nearly whispered, "Don't think I'm crazy, but I think there is a ghost lurking in the shadows and I think he is trying to tell me something."

Rebecca squelched a smirk and deadpan serious asked, "A ghost? Why would you think that?"

"Like I said, just weird things that have been happening to me the past couple of days. Unexplainable things."

"Like what?" Rebecca pressed.

Seemingly on cue, Meghan's long-stemmed glass fell over, on its own, its wet contents dashing across the middle of the table. The women looked at each other with wide eyes.

"Um, something like that?" Rebecca asked, hesitantly.

Taking a moment to respond, Meghan finally said, "Um, well, I think one of us must have bumped the table. That's why it fell over," trying to convince herself more than Rebecca.

"Then why didn't mine fall over, too?"

Meghan shrugged and started mopping up the liquid, trying not to lose her composure, but was visibly shaking.

The place was so noisy that nobody noticed the commotion, but Meghan thought she heard the piano again, though she had a clear view of it and nobody was seated at it.

"Did you hear that?" Meghan asked.

"Hear what?" Rebecca asked.

"You didn't hear the piano, like someone ran their fingers across the length of the keys?"

"No, I sure didn't."

"You don't believe any of this, do you?"

"Actually, I do," Rebecca said. "I just don't want to believe. We've had some recent incidents lately at the nursing home that can't be explained either. I didn't believe at first until I witnessed some of it myself. Now I'm just not sure what to make of all of it. Others definitely are convinced and I'm starting to believe, too."

"I'm telling you, something or someone is trying to tell me, or maybe even us, something," Meghan said.

Rebecca stared at her momentarily, then waved the waitress over.

"I think we're going to need another round," Rebecca said.

SUNDAY, APRIL 14

Harrison slept in and then spent most of the morning lounging in his room. He already could tell that Mug's Pub was going to become a habit. That was not necessarily a bad thing. It was a charming place. Even better, it appeared to be the top place to find out information, without even having to ask.

"There are loose lips here, I just need to pry them open a bit more," Harrison told himself.

He didn't have much on his agenda for the day. He made a notation in his black leather-bound notebook. He had been writing down every detail of what he had seen so far and also described everyone he had encountered.

He also described the silly hodgepodge of stuff that adorned the walls of Mug's Pub. He wondered what that was all about anyway. He described the brick cobblestones of the street, which seemed to match the bricks on the outside wall of his hotel room. The roll-top desk he was seated at was leaned up against the wall, and he faced that wall as he paused in his writing. He noticed a few flaws in the brick and some cracks that followed along some of them. He felt around and one of them shifted slightly out of place. "Interesting," he thought.

After tucking his journal and Amelia's stack of letters to his wife along with the framed family photograph into his hiding place, Harrison went downstairs to the hotel's eating establishment. Brunch was still being served so he had coffee chased by a bloody Mary and loaded up his plate at the buffet—twice. He sat at a table for two in the corner reading today's newspaper. One could learn a lot about a town just from reading the current events. Even the most insignificant item reported in the paper could prove helpful at some later juncture.

He made a mental note to visit the Tirtmansic Historical Society as well.

The hotel dining room was empty save for a couple of families eating together and the waiters and waitresses pretending to look busy. He figured most people were out enjoying the warmth that spring brings after a long, cold and dreary winter. Who could blame them?

Harrison intended to do the same, deciding to head to the park near the river that he had spotted yesterday. He also had seen an excursion boat in the distance and heard a calliope beckoning potential patrons to come aboard and enjoy the view.

Harrison loved discovering a town's character and its people by trying to immerse himself into the scenery, although that didn't seem to be working in Tirtmansic. When he first arrived in a town, he made sure he did all the normal things that people who lived there did, partly to blend in but also so he could gain full experience and knowledge of the place he was researching. The process could be slow but he was the methodical, patient type. It helped him assess the entire situation and make sound decisions on how to advance his plans.

Harrison finished reading the newspaper, drank the last drop of his bloody Mary and headed for the front door. He turned to his left and almost walked straight into the same woman he had held the door open for two nights prior. This time she smiled curtly.

"Thank you, sir," she said. "Aren't you ever so kind? Call me up sometime. I can show your sweet face around town anytime."

Before Harrison could even respond, let alone get her name, she had disappeared quickly inside as if on an important mission.

Harrison strolled down Main Street for about three blocks and then took a left down one of the alleyways, making his way down to the park and riverfront. It already was bustling with Moms and Dads chasing after their rambunctious kids who were determined to get their church clothes dirty. Laughter beckoned him, although the smell of the dirty river wafting his way from a strong breeze almost made him turn and head the other direction. The scent was temporary, or he got used to it, and he kept walking.

When he made it to the park, he decided not to stay as it seemed like a place more for children to play and grown-ups to keep an eye on them. If Penelope was here, they would have been romping along with the rest of the kids. It depressed him to see most of the children frolicking happily with their mothers.

Harrison traveled along the edge of the river, watching its small waves splashing against the gravelly riverbed. The riverboat was not at the dock but he could hear the calliope in the distance and knew it would be back for another excursion soon enough.

He made his way down to the docking area and purchased a ticket for the next cruise, which the ticket seller indicated would depart in an hour.

Harrison was not afraid of being in a floating vessel on a body of water, and in fact had been on several sizes and types of boats in his lifetime. But he always had it in the back of his mind that he would not have anywhere to go but down if the boat capsized or sank. He didn't mind the water so much, particularly in a pool or dipping his feet in the water at the very edge of the ocean, firmly planted on the sandy beach as the water constantly approached and receded.

But being swallowed up into a large body of water, especially a murky river or a lake, where he couldn't see the bottom or what lurked underneath, was not his idea of a good time. Looking down at the brown river water, with the pungent scent lapping at his nose, he knew with absolute certainty that he did not want to end up face first in that.

Yet, Harrison always enjoyed an adventure along with the calm and peace that came with being out on the water. Bodies of water, no matter what size, always helped calm his nerves and contemplate life, or whatever curves it happened to be throwing him at the time. He could be alone with his thoughts and work out some of the more difficult things in life–in his mind anyway.

When it was time for passengers to board for the 2 p.m. excursion, Harrison went up to the top deck and watched the other passengers walk down the gangplank to the boat. He rubbed his hand through his scraggly hair and noted the scruffy developments of a beard and mustache. He contemplated letting at least a mustache form. He would ask Penelope what she thought about that.

When it seemed everyone was on board, one more couple approached: James Thornton and the young woman Harrison had encountered–twice–at the entrance to The Brass Inn.

"This just got fun," Harrison muttered to himself.

Harrison ordered a gin and tonic from the upper deck bar and sat down on one of the wicker deck chairs to enjoy the scenery. He was enjoying the tree-lined river and the architecture that floated by when he caught James Thornton and his lady friend out of the corner of his eye. They had spotted Harrison.

"Afternoon, Mr. Harrison, was it?" Thornton said to Harrison. Harrison stood in deference to the lady and would have offered his hand in a gentlemanly shake but Thornton's arm was occupied with the young lady's right arm firmly entwined in his. Plus, she didn't seem interested in formal social pleasantries.

"Greetings, President Thornton," Harrison said. "Enjoying a nice spring day away from the reminders of daily life?"

Harrison only half-glanced at the young lady, who he could appreciate as being extremely beautiful although she clearly had an attitude. She either did not recognize Harrison from their previous encounters, or chose to pretend she had never seen him. He figured it was the latter but was not sure why.

"Always a pleasure to take in all of the sights that our fine town has to offer," Thornton said. "When you are the president of such a prestigious school as ours, it's important to know everything we have to offer to our visitors in the way of recreation. Please do enjoy your brief stay here and try to take in everything our fine town has to offer before you return to your own."

Harrison focused on the words "sights" and "recreation" and wondered how much Thornton enjoyed such things while his wife was not around.

Thornton left Harrison to his thoughts, wandering away, chuckling to himself, with his lady friend in tow. He had not even had the courtesy of introducing her. Harrison chuckled.

***

After Meghan and Rebecca left Mug's Pub, they were walking across the cobblestone street when Meghan stopped short. Rebecca turned around when she realized Meghan was no longer beside her. She saw Meghan just standing there with a wide-eyed expression.

"What's wrong?" Rebecca asked.

"Did you hear that?"

"Hear what?"

"That clicking sound."

"What clicking sound?"

"The clicking sound every time I walk, the same sound my high heels make when I'm wearing them and walking on the cobblestone street," Meghan said.

"Meghan, your shoes have rubber soles."

"I know. That's the problem. Now it seems like my shoes are clicking but it's not coming from me. It just seems really close to me. Where is that coming from?"

"Your imagination. Too many 'spirits' imbibed at Mug's Pub. I dunno."

"No, seriously," Meghan said. "This same kind of thing has been happening the past couple of days. When I walk down Main Street, I feel like someone's following me and I can hear the clicking. When I turn around, there isn't anyone directly behind me. I thought it was my imagination at first but then I noticed that other people were starting to look at me, almost like they were annoyed because of the sound. I don't know what it is."

"I didn't hear anything. Let's keep walking or we're going to be run over by a car or trampled by a horse."

The women started walking again and Meghan still could hear the clicking noise.

"You seriously don't hear that?"

"All I hear is the clopping of horse hooves. And I don't see anyone following us."

When the women arrived at the end of the street, where the cobblestones gave way to asphalt, the clicking abruptly stopped. Meghan turned around again to see if someone was there but no one was in sight. That was another thing that struck Meghan; that the clicking noise was only apparent when she was walking on the cobblestones or inside the building that housed *The Main Informer*.

As she bid adieu to Rebecca for the evening and got into her vehicle, a sense of uneasiness swept over her. She definitely had been feeling a presence of some sort the past couple of days but this evening, it seemed even more apparent. She could not explain exactly what that presence was but she knew something was out there, along Main Street.

She did not feel threatened but she was anxious about it. And if she told too many people, she might just be committed to the insane asylum, at least, a different type of one from the place she called "work."

MONDAY, APRIL 15, 1912

When Harrison walked into Mug's Pub, he already was feeling somewhat uneasy. The nearly silent restaurant, despite the number of people gathered, made him even more anxious. The people of Tirtmansic were huddled together, whispering to each other, and everyone was reading a copy of the newspaper. Most were gathered together around tables or the bar, two or three sharing a newspaper.

And for the first time, there was no music.

Harrison soon learned what had captured everyone's interest. He opened up his own copy of *The Main Informer* to see for himself. The news was not the same disturbing information that he had just learned. In fact, it appeared that no one here even knew that particular piece of news yet.

However, what he read clearly was devastating.

The largest passenger steamship in the world, the *RMS Titanic*, had sunk in the Atlantic Ocean overnight during its maiden voyage. It was too soon to know how many people had perished but in the coming days, everyone learned that the tragedy had resulted in the deaths of 1,517 of the 2,223 people who had been on board. Only 706 people had survived.

Harrison had just read something about this *Titanic* ship last week. It had been in the news because of its remarkable features and powerful stature, and was expected to arrive on America's shores. He also had heard that some of the high society folks with relatives in the region were going to be passengers on the maiden–and now, final –voyage.

It was hard to imagine how large the ship was and Harrison could not imagine how it could have sunk, and relatively quickly, from initial reports.

Harrison thought back to his own trip on the excursion boat yesterday, which was miniscule in comparison.

"What was I worried about?" he muttered.

After reading some of the details, he shuddered to think about how dark the night must have been, and how frigid the ocean water was. He figured that most people did not have time to think the same types of thoughts he normally thought in anticipation of being tossed to the waters. In fact, the only thought going through most of their minds probably was survival. Or worse, their fear likely stemmed from not knowing when death might take them.

In the coming days and weeks and months, everyone would learn how the ship that some had perceived as unsinkable actually sank after hitting an iceberg. There was some debate about how fast the vessel was going and how there were not enough lifeboats on board to save all the passengers from their watery grave. But the ship actually had more lifeboats on board than the law of the day required. The law later was changed due to the tragedy. However, the crew failed to fill up the lifeboats to full capacity, which had been tested to hold 70 large, adult men without problems. But the ship's crew didn't know that and feared that sending the boats down the side of the *Titanic* and into the ocean with more than 20 or 30 people certainly would result in them cracking apart mid-air.

The crew had decided to err on the side of caution and thus ran out of enough room to evacuate everyone from the large ship.

After reading some of the early details of the tragedy, the people of Tirtmansic started realizing that they might know some of the passengers. They frantically scanned the articles, searching for any possible names of survivors, somebody who might be quoted, just to know that their friend or loved one had been among those who lived.

While everyone else was stunned and focused on the *Titanic* tragedy, Harrison had a different kind of sinking feeling.

And he knew that the latest revelation was going to temporarily delay his intended mission for the day, to meet the woman behind Annabelle Adams' School for Young Ladies. Mrs. Amelia Adams Thornton had started the school and then married this James Thornton character. Her mistake was making him the president of the school.

Prior to leaving his hotel room, Harrison had received a written message under his door. He did not know for certain if the message was legitimate. But if it was true, it would upend and completely change his investigation.

He needed to share the news with the one person he trusted, as soon as possible.

APRIL 15, 1992

Meghan was sitting at her desk, alone. It was quiet save for an abandoned radio humming nearby. She could hear the faint sounds of the horse-drawn carriages and cars navigating their way side-by-side down Main Street. Thankfully, she thought, the calliope always went silent by 5 p.m. each day.

It was not unusual for Meghan to receive gifts of some sort with certain press releases. Some were quirky and some were useful, like fancy pens with a company's name embossed on them. Sometimes she received food and had a difficult time hiding that from the newsroom. They had an uncanny sense of food walking in the door as soon as it arrived.

Ad agencies and PR firms used these gifts as a way to stand out and have their press releases noticed. If an editor or reporter remembered the unique manner in which they received the press release, there was a better chance of having their information published.

Technically, the newspaper had a policy in which reporters and editors were not allowed to accept gifts or free lunches, as they could be viewed as bribes. But the unspoken rationale among the staff was that the meager salary barely paid for a burger and ice cream cone at Dairy Queen. The boss also made it clear that he didn't want to see lunches on the paper's expense account. So while he didn't encourage the practice, his theory was that if someone else would pick up the check, the less he had to worry about from a financial perspective. And if you shared the gifts and goodies that arrived, particularly the food, with others, they ignored the fact that anyone received anything.

Meghan's latest acquisition intrigued her, mostly because it was announcing that an exhibit of artifacts recovered from the *Titanic* would be visiting a neighboring town for three weeks. The press kit contained a mock "boarding pass" to get onto the "ship" at the exhibit hall. It listed a real passenger's name and told her that she would be "staying" in second class during her brief "voyage." The press kit also contained a miniature replica of the *Titanic* ship and a box of assorted teas and scones. She was surprised that the scones were still on her desk.

Without warning, the fake boarding pass blew out of her hand and landed on the floor next to the exterior wall of her office. For a second it appeared that the pass was suspended in air.

Meghan hadn't felt a gust of air. Her window wasn't open and the door had not moved. She chalked it up to the air conditioning kicking on and creating a wind gust.

At least, that is what she told herself had just happened.

She bent down to pick up the piece of paper, which had landed at the base of the wall. She noticed how the once pristine-white wall now held a dirty-white hue.

She also noticed a small hole in the old wood floor, which creaked from age when she stepped on it. She pondered whether the errant pass might have been pointing her to something underneath. With some effort, she pried up part of the floorboard, but nothing was there.

CHAPTER 8

Meghan started each work day with her morning coffee and a stack of newspapers. She not only wrote for and read *The Main Informer,* she kept up on other publications and current events. Knowledge was everything in her line of work.

After receiving the unique *Titanic* press release, she began reading again about the tragedy. She was in awe of how many people had died. She also was in awe of some of the stories of bravery, and the will to survive.

The whole tragedy made her ask her favorite question about everything, "Why?" And then she wondered, "Why were some people saved while others did not make it?"

While perusing one of the newspapers that detailed the *Titanic* tragedy, she noticed a brief news item about a tragedy closer to home. The story indicated that there either had been a homicide or suspicious disappearance of the owner of a school for girls. A man named Harrison Parker was listed as an investigator of some sort. She later learned that this Harrison fellow had been investigating the man prior to his death or disappearance. The school owner–or his body - evidently had never been found.

The only reason the story caught her eye was the fact that the investigator's name was Harrison Parker. When she came in to work that morning, a sticky note was affixed to her computer screen. In black marker, written, in a scrawled, man's handwriting, the note said, "I can lead you to the truth about Harrison Parker."

She asked some of the folks in the newsroom if they had written the note or if they knew what it meant. Everyone appeared oblivious, and even disinterested. She wondered how someone had gotten up to the second floor, past the bulldog of a receptionist, and how nobody noticed someone leaving something on her desk.

The fact that Meghan had just read about a Harrison Parker and she had received this message was not a coincidence. She felt the need to learn more about this Harrison's initial investigation and why he was interested in the school's owner. She couldn't explain it but had an odd feeling that she needed to find out more about this mystery, and if it had anything to do with the other odd incidents lately.

Meghan dug the crumpled sticky note out of her trash bin and placed it below the computer screen. She rang up Diane at the Tirtmansic Historical Society and asked if she could find out more about what was described in the initial article.

After she got up and was at the door of her office, the light bulb hovering over her desk suddenly crashed down, shattering into millions of slivers. Everyone in the place stood in momentary shock before someone ran in to start cleaning up the mess. Meghan was too shaken to move.

APRIL 17, 1912

Harrison met his partner, Lance Cutter, at the train station. The old comrades shook hands in greeting. The dark-haired Harrison towered over his longtime partner and friend, who had more grey hair peeking out through his sandy blond buzz cut everyday.

"Well, well, well," Cutter said. "I let you go on a solo mission for once and you go and mess it all up. That's usually my specialty, ol' pal."

"I didn't mess anything up. Someone else messed things up," Harrison said. "My plan was moving along just fine and at my normal, patient pace. Someone else decided to speed things up."

"Well, let's get started," Cutter said. "Take me to the hotel so I can wash up and we'll go have a bite to eat and digest this news."

Harrison led his only trusted friend to the waiting taxi in front of the train station. When Cutter stepped out of the cab in front of The Brass Inn, he did not notice anything extraordinary about the place. But when he walked into the lobby, he couldn't help but let out an approving whistle.

"Is this on the expense account? You've maxed it out for the whole department if so, old buddy," Cutter said.

"What can I say? It's cheaper than the five-star hotels the chief stays in when he goes to New York and Florida for his 'training' sessions," Harrison said sarcastically. "Besides, if I'm going to play the part, I must look the part, digs included. It's all part of the job."

"The chief's not going to be happy when he finds out we're both charging the department for these digs," Cutter said.

Harrison laughed and said, "So you want your own room or do you want to keep the costs down and sleep on the floor in my room?"

"I actually have seniority *and* rank over you so it would be your ass on the floor," Cutter said, deadpan but knowing his partner was not offended. "I'll take my chances with the chief's 10-minute tirade to avoid sleeping with you, let alone on the floor."

With keys in hand, Harrison went to his room at the end of the hallway while Cutter opened the door across the hall. Harrison said he was going to call Penelope and they agreed to meet in front of The Brass Inn in 15 minutes.

It was past breakfast time but too early for lunch so the duo strolled down to the opposite end of Main Street in search of a combination of the two meals.

"Now I know why they call it brunch," Cutter chuckled. His partner didn't laugh. In fact he seemed deep in thought.

Harrison purposely walked along the east side of the street so they would not pass directly in front of Mug's Pub. He would introduce Lance to the establishment some other time.

He also decided he should broaden his meal options and eat elsewhere for a change. He remembered that Woodson mentioned a place on the south end of the street. The Tilted Teapot's atmosphere was quite different from Mug's Pub, a bright place with an open floor plan in an old warehouse. Despite the three levels that were connected with wrought-iron staircases, it seemed more like a cafeteria.

They requested a private booth in a corner and the hostess led them to a table on the second level, which seemed to be the main dining area. There were only five other tables occupied out of the 20 or so in the room and she seated them at the booth furthest from the rest of the diners.

Harrison loved small-town accommodation.

"So what's good here, partner?" Cutter asked.

"Never eaten here but word is that it's all good. Cooking seems to be a specialty of this little town."

Once their orders were placed and the steam from the coffee was rising into their faces, Cutter said, "So what the hell happened? Start from the beginning."

Harrison described in detail everything he had done and the people he had encountered since he arrived in town.

"And this note that you received, where is it now?"

"I have it in a safe place with other things related to the investigation. I want you to take it back with you to have the lab rats analyze it for fingerprints, the usual drill."

"What does it say?"

"'I know who you are and why you are here. Go away. Your work is done here. Thornton's dead.' It's clearly a man's handwriting. I've only been using my real first name but nobody knows what I do for a living. They don't even know where I came from or why I am here. They think I'm here to look at the school for Penelope's education."

"And no scuttlebutt so far that Thornton's actually dead, or has anyone even noticed that he's not around?" Cutter asked.

"Nothing. I asked one of the taxi drivers, the one who drove us earlier, if he had heard of anything strange happening the last couple of days and all he knew was about the *Titanic*," Harrison said. "That's all anyone has talked about since it happened. Nobody seems to be concerned that there may have been a murder of one of the most prominent members of the town. And nobody misses him because he was scheduled to be out on a business trip until tomorrow anyway."

"So the townsfolk are oblivious to the potential danger in their own back yards," Cutter said. "But is anyone else in physical danger? This guy is a scheister, after all. He is the one who has a natural target on his back. And how do we know he's even dead?"

"I don't know the answer to any of that," Harrison said. "The citizens all have the local authorities and newspaper reporters focused on finding out if any of their rich friends and neighbors are among the living or dead from that shipwreck. They are so busy combing through the wire news services and trying to reach friends of friends of friends in New York that they could care less about anything else. There's so little real crime in this town that the authorities and newspaper publishers are loving that they have something big finally to cover, even though it's not a local story."

"I don't want to go to the local authorities about this because then your cover is completely blown and I don't want them knowing about this investigation," Cutter said. "They likely wouldn't like out-of-town detectives snooping in their business. From what you said you learned before you came here, I'm sure they are in pretty tight with our boy Thornton anyway. I have no doubt in a small town like this that they've been paid a pretty penny to make sure any sort of investigation of Thornton never happens."

The waitress reappeared with their breakfasts and topped off their coffees without even asking, then walked away just as silently as she had appeared.

Cutter lowered his voice and said, "Are you sure you want to continue with all of this? It has the potential to be more dangerous than you initially thought if murder is involved. We initially thought this was some sort of fraud involving money and government bribes."

Without hesitating, Harrison responded, "I am more determined than ever to get to the bottom of this. Plus, I would not be able to live with myself if Madeline's friend is in danger and I didn't do anything to try to protect her. I need to do this for Madeline."

Cutter knew not to argue with his partner; Harrison was stubborn and when it came to his wife, there was absolutely no room for negotiation. Cutter sighed and said, "OK. I'm going to stick around for a couple of days just to make sure things don't get crazy."

"Isn't Chief Do-Nothing going to miss you?" Harrison said with his charming sarcastic tone.

"I told him I was sick and you know how he is about anyone coming to work with even a sniffle," Cutter said. "He'll allow criminals to wander free on the streets but his own employees are scum of the earth if they bring germs into his kingdom."

Both chuckled and finished their breakfasts.

They wandered back out onto Main Street and Harrison stopped one of the horse-and-buggy cabs to drive them around the downtown/Main Street area so his partner could see the town for himself. The slow ride was a good distraction for Harrison to think while Cutter took in the sights. Each of them would notice and point out things that the other missed.

That was one of the reasons the duo was such a good detective team. When one noticed something, the other would notice something different. When one faltered, the other would pick up the slack.

That afternoon, Harrison called his driver friend to take them to Annabelle Adams' School for Young Ladies. He figured he might as well pay Thornton's wife a visit despite the latest developments. First, he could scope out if anything was amiss at the school or if she had any inkling of Thornton's fate. He also figured that Thornton had not bothered to tell his wife about his visit on Saturday so his presence would be a surprise.

CHAPTER 10

Harrison's wife, Madeline, had died nearly a year before he embarked on his mission to this quaint Midwest town with the funny name. His beloved had passed away when she was seven months pregnant. Their second daughter, Brooke, had lived for three days after birth but also died from complications due to being delivered two months early.

Harrison was devastated. Madeline was his world; she was so full of life and vigor, a contrast to his sometimes melancholy and stoic personality. He was looking forward to having a second clone of Madeline in the house, filling it with laughter and giggles and bright-eyed smiles from all three of the beautiful ladies he would cherish.

Harrison was so heartbroken that he could barely take care of his other daughter, Penelope, although Harrison called her Sweet Pea in her presence.

Her smile and innocent face reminded him so much of Madeline and he was sure that Brooke would have been exactly the same. His heart ached for Penelope's loss almost more than it ached for himself. How was a child, a daughter, supposed to grow up without a mother? She did not fully understand that there was a baby in her mama's belly but she understood the concept of having a baby brother or sister to love. And now neither her mother nor her promised baby sister were here to cherish.

After a few months of struggling and always eating at Madeline's parents' house anyway, they had offered to take care of Penelope for a while so that he could mend his heart.

"You need to make yourself healthy before you can even begin to take care of your daughter," Madeline's mother had told him, in a caring, motherly way. "You can spend all day and night here with her if you want or you can take a couple of days for yourself if needed. Just feel confident that she is being taken care of and loved and cherished all the time."

Truth be told, Harrison knew he was not being the best father to his Sweet Pea.

He couldn't get through the fog of his own suffering. Her bright brown eyes and blonde ringlets reminded him so much of his wife, and her laughter brought a smile to his face regardless of how bad a mood he might be in. He turned to mush in her presence. But the light mood faded when Penelope wasn't with him.

Except for this current little excursion, Harrison had not been away from Penelope since Madeline died. His routine consisted of work, then stopping at his in-laws' home for dinner every night, reading to Penelope and tucking her into bed, often dozing alongside her. He would share breakfast with Penelope and her grandparents before heading off to work again. He felt blessed to have such caring in-laws.

One night while lying in bed, Penelope looked up at her father and asked, with all the innocence of a 6-year-old, "Daddy, are Mommy and Brooke watching and listening to us everyday?"

Harrison fought back the tears and tried to comfort his daughter.

"Sweet Pea, they're with us all the time, right here in our hearts and our minds," Harrison said, pointing to her chest and head to illustrate. "They will be with us forever, guiding us in everything we do. Anytime you feel lonely or sad or need your Mommy or sister, you can talk to them."

"Will they hear me?"

"They will hear you but they won't be able to answer back," Harrison said, trying to give his daughter some peace without giving her too much hope for something that was never going to happen. "Just know that they are tucked safely into a special place in your heart and will be with us always that way."

Harrison also grabbed the photo off her nightstand of the three of them, taken just two weeks before Madeline died.

"Keep this as a reminder of your Mommy and how happy she was to have you as her daughter," Harrison said. "She loved you very much. Don't ever forget that, my dear Sweet Pea."

Penelope smiled the Madeline smile and then looked at her father and said, "She loved you very much, too, Daddy. She told me that all the time and I even heard her say it out loud when you weren't home."

Harrison leaned over to hug his daughter goodnight so he could hide the tears forming in the corners of his eyes. He mustered up enough bravery to say, "Sleep well, my angel. Have only sweet dreams." Harrison then turned off the light and lay in the darkness holding his daughter in his arms until he heard her steady breathing of sleep.

CHAPTER 11

Not long after the bedtime conversation with Penelope, he found the distraction he was looking for among some of Madeline's paperwork. He discovered letters from a friend, Amelia, that seemed to come to Madeline on a frequent basis.

Harrison vaguely recalled Madeline talking about her friend Amelia, who had started a school for young ladies. Madeline and Amelia had gone to finishing school and a teaching college together and had their love of children and education as a common bond. He didn't recall many details beyond that except that Madeline occasionally would relate some tidbit of news from Amelia's letters praising this child or that for something they had accomplished and how happy Amelia was to see these children's brains growing each year.

Madeline had taught pre-schoolers how to read and thoroughly enjoyed spending time with the children, even the unruly ones. He could never figure out how she had so much patience because sometimes the babbling children would start to drive him right out of his mind.

Madeline never had the ambitions that Amelia had of starting her own school, but felt that she had a lot to offer to a small group of children, giving them a good foundation with reading skills.

Harrison started to read the letters simply as a way to feel close to Madeline. He thought they might spark some sort of memory or moment in time that he could recall, or maybe never knew about Madeline. It was his warped way of feeling like he could reconnect with her and keep her memory alive.

But he found more than just tidbits about his wife, which inevitably made him smile or laugh.

Harrison read the letters from Amelia over and over again, to the point of near obsession.

Amelia clearly was distressed and it appeared to be because of her husband, who she had married five years earlier. According to her letters, the school was in dire financial straits even though Amelia knew that the school was making money. The town government was involved in some way as well but it wasn't clear in her letters if that was connected to her husband's dealings or a result of her own activism, or both.

She mentioned enlisting the help of a couple of "close allies" in her letters but did not say who it was. She had asked Madeline to send all correspondence via her friend Frank Henderson, care of an establishment called Mug's Pub, fearing her husband might intercept the correspondence because he always retrieved the contents of the school's letterbox before she could get to it herself. The return address on the letters had the initials A.A.A., care of Mug's Pub, 221 N. Main Street, in Tirtmansic.

Because he basically had been living at Madeline's parents' house, Harrison had let almost everything go at his own homestead. He started sifting through all the mail that had been piling up on his roller-top desk and discovered more letters from Amelia, ones that were sent after Madeline passed away. They all had gone unanswered and each one sounded more desperate than the previous ones, mainly because Amelia had not received any correspondence in return.

After pondering this woman's plight for a while, Harrison felt the need to do something. He not only felt a pull to find someone who was close to Madeline so he could still feel her presence in his heart; he also felt the pull of the mystery behind the letters. He could feel the desperation bleeding through the ink and paper.

He wanted to find out more and perhaps help his wife's friend, if he could.

He needed a break from his life right now anyway. This might be just the thing, to go to a different town and solve someone else's problems.

First, Harrison had to concoct some story for the police chief about something happening in this sleepy little town that was related to an investigation back home. That way, he could get the chief to pay for his travel expenses, Harrison concluded. It probably wasn't ethical but the chief always used more than his share of the monthly expense account for his so-called business trips.

The chief happily obliged because Harrison's downtrodden mood was depressing him and the rest of the department. He didn't even care or ask about the details because truth be told, the chief had no clue what his underlings did on a day-to-day basis. He spent his time glad-handing politicians and the movers and shakers, and as long as his boys stayed out of major trouble – and the headlines – they could do whatever they wanted as far as he was concerned. He just didn't want to be bothered with the minor, petty details.

"Just don't get into any trouble and keep our department's name clean," the chief had barked at Harrison as he walked out of the office.

"Yeah, yeah, yeah," Harrison had muttered to himself, knowing full well how the department always needed to maintain a polished reputation, despite the real crime going on in the confines of the police station.

Harrison's partner, Lance Cutter, knew the real reason Harrison was going to Tirtmansic. They had been partners for a decade and he also thought Harrison needed a slight distraction and time away from everything that reminded him of his wife, if only for a little while. Although, he was walking straight into the path of his wife's memory. But Cutter thought it might help Harrison find some closure if he spent some time with a woman who had known his wife in a previous lifetime.

Cutter secretly wanted in on the investigation but he wasn't interested in all the details. He would help his old pal with anything he needed but he also needed to keep up appearances back home and keep the chief from nosing around too much about Harrison's doings.

Of course, Cutter also knew that the chief liked Harrison and his own paranoia made him think that the chief completely despised Cutter. Somehow, even though they both were rebels, Harrison always came out smelling like a rose while Cutter ended up in the chief's doghouse.

The chief had some sympathy for Harrison; he didn't know what the hell Cutter's problem was beyond being a major thorn in his side.

The worst part for Harrison was telling his Sweet Pea that he needed to go away for a few days. She cried and wailed and screamed.

"First Mommy went away and took Brooke with her and now you're going, too," Penelope shouted at him, gasping for breath between her big tears. "Everyone's leaving me."

Harrison spent three days talking to Penelope, reassuring her that he was only going away for a brief work trip. The only difference was that he wouldn't be able to come home for dinner and to tuck her in for a few days. He reassured her that her grandparents would tend to her every need and he promised to call her five times a day and read to her at bedtime, even if it was over the phone.

In reality, he probably was calling her 10 times a day. She regaled him with her playful activities of the day. He missed her so much and told her all the time how much he loved her and would be home soon.

He would hang up with tears in his eyes and apologize to her for not being there for her, holding her through her own grief. She was young but understood enough to know that her mother was not coming back. She hoped that her Daddy returned.

When he had left for this trip, Penelope told him to wait a minute and ran up to her room at her grandparents' house. She came back and silently handed the family photograph to him.

"You are going to need this more than me right now so take it with you, Daddy," Penelope said as she leaned in to hug him.

It was the last photograph that had been taken of his family, the one of Harrison, Madeline and Penelope together with Madeline's big belly looking like it was about to explode from the baby growing inside. She was almost seven months pregnant at the time of the photo; just two weeks before she went into an unexplainable coma and never woke up.

Penelope did not know it, but tucked behind the photograph, inside the frame, was a photo of Brooke as a 1-day-old baby. He had not showed the photo to Penelope yet because he feared it would be too traumatic for her at her tender age.

Harrison did not necessarily need the photographs to remind him of their beautiful faces; he carried them in his heart. But he could not deny this loving gesture from his daughter and it did give him comfort to carry a tangible reminder of all three of his girls.

CHAPTER 12

When the driver dropped Harrison and Cutter off at the entrance to the school, Harrison noticed more young ladies outside in the fresh air than on his previous visit. There appeared to be teachers supervising the well-behaved girls.

As they walked up the roadway toward the tables full of girls, one woman separated herself from the groups and walked over to greet them.

"May I help you, gentlemen?" she said with a cautious but pleasant smile.

"Hello, my name is Harrison, pleased to meet you, ma'am," Harrison said. "This is my brother, Lance. I came by on Saturday to inquire about schooling for my young daughter and a Mr. Thornton suggested I come by to inquire of the young lady whose name adorns the school."

"I am Amelia Adams, pleased to meet you," Amelia said, offering her hand in greeting. "We are just about finished with our afternoon lessons and the young ladies will be sent to their rooms to wash up and prepare for their supper. Perhaps you would like to stroll the grounds for 10 minutes and meet me on the porch of the building straight ahead. I will have our servant prepare some tea and biscuits."

Harrison did not know it at the time, but when he came face-to-face with the woman on this day, she turned out to be the same woman who had been sitting alone at the bar the first time he walked into Mug's Pub. It made sense to him now that she would be there, in that establishment. She obviously trusted the proprietor and must have felt comfortable going there.

From the settee on the porch, Harrison and Cutter watched the women wrap up their lessons and disperse the young ladies to their dormitory. Amelia spoke to some of the teachers. She seemingly commanded a great deal of respect from them as they listened intently to her instructions.

Then Amelia made her way up to see to her guests. They both rose to greet her.

"Welcome, gentlemen," Amelia said. "Please, sit. Our tea should be here momentarily. Did you hear about the tragedy of the *Titanic*? How terribly awful for everyone on that ship. I cannot even imagine how frigid the water was and how horrifying it was to see your ship just sink into the ocean and vanish in the dark of night."

"My wife wanted to be on that ship," Cutter said. "She talked about it incessantly. I, unfortunately, do not have the means on my meager salary to afford such a trip. For the first time in my life, I think I am grateful for that fact."

The three chatted a little more about the miniscule tidbits each had been able to glean from the news reports on what exactly happened. They discussed how there may not have been enough lifeboats to save everyone and how long it took after the S.O.S. distress signal for other ships to reach the wreckage in time to rescue the people.

When the conversation seemed to fade, Amelia asked, "So, you said your name is Harrison?"

"Yes, ma'am, the one and only," Harrison said, smiling, almost flirting with the stunning woman sitting in the chair across from them.

"I have a dear friend named Madeline whose husband is named Harrison. It's only the second time in my life that I have heard that name," Amelia said.

"Well, ma'am, I am the one and only Harrison, Harrison Parker, as a matter of fact," he said, this time with a glint of sadness returning to his eyes upon hearing Madeline's name spoken out loud.

"Oh, well, what a pleasure to meet the man I have heard so much about," Amelia said. "I have been corresponding with Madeline for quite some time but it's been almost a year since I heard from her. Is she with you on your trip? I so would love to see her and also want to meet your beautiful daughter. She has written so much about you and Penelope. She also had written about the impending birth of your second child in her letters. Did you end up having a boy or girl? She said she didn't care either way because she already loved the baby so much."

Cutter and Harrison shared an uncomfortable look and then Harrison sighed. He knew he would have to muddle through this conversation at some point.

"I am sorry to be the one to tell you, but my dear wife died nearly a year ago," Harrison said, feeling the tears forming and trying to compose himself. "She fell into a coma while she was seven months pregnant and our daughter, Brooke, was delivered prematurely but only survived for three days."

Cutter jumped in quickly, seeing his friend starting to fall apart, "Harrison just recently found your letters and wanted to come here to tell you in person because he could tell from your letters how close you and Madeline were."

"I would have contacted you or come earlier, but I was so wrapped up in my own grief and taking care of Penelope that I just recently started going through Madeline's things," Harrison said. "That's when I discovered the letters, and all the ones that have been piling up on my desk since she died."

"Oh, good heavens, I had no idea," said Amelia, the news sinking in and she stood up to embrace Harrison in a warm hug. "I knew she was having the baby so I figured she was just so busy with the new baby and taking care of Penelope and you that she had not had time to respond. I kept waiting and checking to see if she had responded, but each day went by with no response. I never even fathomed she could have died."

Amelia sat back down and the reality of the news struck her head-on as she burst into tears. It was Harrison's turn to reach out to her in a warm, comforting embrace. After she regained her composure and could talk in complete sentences, Amelia began treading on a little different territory, a topic she was more comfortable discussing - children.

"How is your daughter, Penelope, doing?" Amelia said. "I know Madeline was so excited when she became pregnant with her and I loved reading her stories of Penelope growing into a young lady. I feel like I already know her without having ever met her. I also feel like I already know you even though we've just met."

"She's an amazing young lady, even for only being 6 years old," Harrison said. "She definitely has her mother's beautiful looks, a great smile and a charming personality."

"She is a little charmer, warms your heart just to be around her," Cutter chimed in.

"Oh, I do hope to meet her soon," Amelia said, brightening just discussing the prospect.

"She is not with me on this trip but I definitely will bring her back," Harrison said. "What about you? Do you have children? I don't recall you referring to any in your letters."

"Aside from the young ladies we teach here, no," Amelia said, almost solemnly.

"Oh, I'm sorry," Harrison said.

"It's wonderful to have all of these girls around me all the time so I don't really notice that much," Amelia said. "I consider all of them my adopted children. I adore and love all of them as if they were my own. They bring great joy and fulfillment to my life."

Harrison wanted to broach the subject of her husband but didn't know how to politely change the subject to official business. At the same time, something suddenly dawned on Amelia.

"Oh, horrors, you have read my letters?" Amelia said.

Harrison hesitated and said, "Yes, ma'am, I have."

Amelia scrunched up her nose and then said, "Oh, my," for lack of anything else to say and lowered her eyes. "So you know all about my husband, James." A statement, not a question.

"Well, only what is in the letters," Harrison said. "I am sure there is more to the story but from what I could figure out, you are not deserving of having this man in your life."

There was a pause and then Harrison jumped in quickly and said, "I mean no offense, ma'am. I just want you to know that you can trust me as much as you trusted Madeline. I am the only other person who has read your letters and they are tucked away in a safe place. I have shared some of the contents with Lance here but he has not read them. Lance and I are detectives. I am a police detective and he is Sergeant Detective Lance Cutter, but we prefer it if you keep that quiet for the time being. We don't want to alert the local authorities that we're stomping on their turf. If I can explain, Lance isn't my brother, in a blood relation sense. But I trust him like he is my brother. I trust him with my life."

Amelia looked at both men, somewhat bewildered and not sure how to feel or react. She started to speak but no words could come out.

"I want to assure you, Amelia, that we are here to try to help you," Harrison said. "It is true that I possibly am going to enroll my daughter here because she needs a good education and I cannot provide that in my current mental state. I know Madeline had a tremendous amount of respect for you as an educator and aside from Madeline, you are the only other woman I think I would trust teaching her."

Amelia smiled a sweet smile in acknowledgement before Harrison continued.

"But I also wanted to come to see what I can do to help you."

Amelia hesitated and then said, reluctantly, "Well, then we should probably go somewhere a little more private to have this conversation."

With that, Amelia stood up and the two men followed. They

walked down the building's front steps toward the administrative building where Harrison originally met Thornton. Amelia was walking slightly ahead of the two men but turned around, noted the noise emanating from Harrison's right heel, yet declined to say anything. Cutter also gave Harrison a curious look.

Harrison grinned and said, "Yeah, I know, I need to go to the shoe cobbler and get that fixed. Been meaning to do it all week."

Amelia just smiled politely and kept walking.

She led them into an office just short of Thornton's. She quietly shut the door and showed the men to the two chairs facing her desk. Amelia walked around to the opposite side and sat down before the men took their seats.

"Let me start by saying that I trusted your wife with my life, just as you say you trust your partner here with yours," Amelia said. "I also trust, obviously, Frank, who owns Mug's Pub, which is why my correspondence to your wife was being funneled through his place. He has been like a father to me and has been willing to help me in any way possible. He and his piano man keep their eyes and ears open for me."

"Would that be Robert Woodson?" Harrison asked.

"Yes, do you know him?" Amelia said.

"Yes, I heard him play the first night I was here and I had breakfast with him the next day," Harrison said. "I also have met Frank but have not had much opportunity to have a meaningful conversation with either one."

"I trust Robert and Frank completely, and they know what is going on. They have been helping me with several of the matters that I alluded to in my letters," Amelia said. "I want to trust both of you but you'll have to forgive me for being skeptical. I trusted my husband, too. I trusted him so much that I stupidly turned the business affairs of the school over to him after two years of marriage. In just three years, he has managed to almost completely upend everything I have devoted my life to building."

Amelia paused and then went on.

"I do not want any of the girls or the teachers or their parents or anyone in the community to know what is going on, beyond those who already know, and that is Frank and Robert, and one other individual," Amelia said. "I have been doing some of my own detective work. My husband believes that I am a young, naïve woman who needs to depend on a man to run her business. Yes, I was naïve about him but I am on to him now and I do not need him to become suspicious or get any inkling that I am spying on him so I can figure out how to repair the damage that he has done. In that respect, your secret of being detectives also is safe with me."

Harrison did not want to alarm her about Thornton possibly being murdered and the fact that a killer might be at-large. Instead, he said, "Where is Mr. Thornton right now?"

Harrison and Cutter both detected a hint of a smirk before Amelia said, "Officially, he is on a business trip, some governmental affairs or something. But I already know that that is not the case. At this very moment, he probably is with his mistress at the brothel she owns, or with some other floozy."

Amelia said it like she didn't care that her husband was keeping company with other women.

Harrison knew something was awry with this Thornton fellow but did not know this tidbit. He also tried to hide his surprise at how matter-of-fact Amelia had stated this news, which had to be humiliating and embarrassing for such a prim, proper lady.

"A brothel?" Harrison said.

"That's what I said," Amelia said. "I discovered his business dealings with this place when I was snooping through his desk. He has no idea that I have keys to all of his office doors, desk drawers and closets. Like I said, I'm not as stupid or as naïve as I may appear."

CHAPTER 13

Harrison took Cutter to his new watering hole, Mug's Pub, for a nightcap. Nobody was in the place except Frank, and the piano player, who was sitting at the bar having his own nightcap.

"Evening, fellas," Harrison said as he walked in like he had been going to the place for years.

"Good evening, Harrison, how are you on this fine evening?" Frank greeted him with a smile and a nod toward his partner. "Welcome to Mug's Pub. What can I get fer you chaps tonight?"

Harrison ordered a gin and tonic and Cutter went for the less toxic beer.

Harrison introduced Cutter to Frank and Robert and took a seat next to Woodson, even though it meant he had his back to the rest of the pub. But then again, nobody else was in the place. Cutter sat on the other side of Harrison.

Frank served up the beverages and poured himself a bourbon. He raised his glass to the other three men and said "Bottoms up!"

"This *Titanic* thing has everyone in a frenzy," Frank said. "We're usually slow early in the week but things usually pick up as the week progresses. So what are you two up to tonight?"

"Not much. We had a visit with Amelia Adams about enrolling my daughter in the school," Harrison said. "Seems like a pleasant young woman."

Frank and Robert exchanged glances, then Robert said, "Vey nice young lady. She is doing great things teaching those young ladies. She also is actively involved in the community, always helping with a charity or giving a lift to someone less fortunate. It's not just her, either. It's all of them at the school, well except one. They all get involved in the community, from the servants to the students and the teachers all the way up to Amelia. Always willing to lend a hand and make their little piece of the earth better for everyone."

Frank took another sip of his drink and had a pensive look as if he was agreeing, then started scrubbing at imagined dirt with his dish towel.

"I know it's only the four of us sitting here tonight, but how 'bout you show my friend here what a master you are with that instrument?" Harrison said to Robert.

"Be happy to oblige," Woodson said, as he stepped away from his stool, tipped his empty glass toward Frank in a silent request for a refill and plopped himself onto the piano bench.

Without even looking at the keys, Woodson looked out at his audience and belted out a few tunes. No sheet music, no need to look down even once. His fingers knew the songs before his brain even told them what to do. He played songs such as Scott Joplin's "Maple Leaf Rag" and "The Entertainer," Irving Berlin's "Alexander's Ragtime Band," and the popular "Come Josephine in my Flying Machine," among others.

Cutter was just as impressed as Harrison. Apparently others had heard the faint sounds of the music from the street, because slowly the bar started filling up with patrons and eventually every bar stool, chair and booth was filled.

When he could catch a break from serving everyone without extra wait staff to help, Frank poured Harrison and Cutter refills on their drinks and said "Tonight's tab is on the house, for bringing all of these customers in just by suggesting that Robert play the piano."

After several more rounds – Harrison and Cutter both lost count – they stumbled out of the front of Mug's Pub and managed to click their way up to The Brass Inn.

"Will you get that dang shoe repaired, Parker?" Cutter slurred to his partner.

Harrison chuckled.

"Women love it. Didn't you see how it got Amelia's attention? And all those women who flocked to the bar? That was because of me, they've heard me all over town!"

"Right, dream on little buddy," Cutter said. "That would annoy any woman."

"My friend, women pretend to be annoyed but our quirks are what charm them," Harrison said. "They need something to 'fix' so they look for our faults and weaknesses and hone in on them. Then once they are well into their makeover projects, we have them hooked on us, flaws and all."

Cutter opened the front door to The Brass Inn, rolled his eyes and stumbled up the steps to his room to pass out. He could still hear Harrison's chuckling as he fell asleep.

CHAPTER 14

Harrison and Cutter were doing what they do best: surveillance. They had been on hundreds of reconnaissance missions during their time as partners and had become friends over the years because of it. They had to do something to whittle away the hours so two men who didn't do much talking found it easier to fill the time with talk about their lives or about absolutely nothing than to sit in silence.

They had secured a vehicle and found "Wild Stallions," the brothel on the outskirts of town. After parking in a secluded spot, they walked through the dark night to stake out a good place to watch the comings and goings at the establishment.

The air was cooler than during the day and especially under cover of the ominous trees swaying above them.

"This could be a long night, are you sure you don't need a blankie and time to get your beauty sleep?" Harrison teased his partner.

"I'm not the one pouring the drinks down with your new friends at Mug's," Cutter retorted. "Perhaps you should take a nap while I stand guard."

Harrison pressed his finger to his lips to tell Cutter to hush. The air had been still, quiet save for the rustling of leaves in the trees hanging above and some distant animals stalking in the night. They had done this duty for so long they practically breathed in tandem, silently communicating their thoughts with a glance or hand gesture.

Cutter gave a puzzled look. Harrison listened for a while and then shook his head as if to say "all clear." Then the two focused on their target.

Wild Stallions was what most proper people referred to as a place of ill repute. Harrison and Cutter could see through the thin curtains on the lower level of the house that men were drinking and smoking cigars or cigarettes while ladies in fancy get-ups bounced from one patron to another, all the while flirting, flipping their hair and laughing at the appropriate times. Upstairs, the rooms were darker but some light peeked through the heavier curtains. Only slight shadows could be detected.

Both men had been in enough of these types of places in their lifetimes – as investigators, mostly, or so they liked to tell people – to know the general layout and rules of engagement.

From their viewpoint, Harrison and Cutter could not specifically identify the patrons but didn't really care.

One particular woman, a buxom redhead, caught their eye, though. She seemed to be keeping the place hopping, always wandering around the main living area of the house, checking on her guests and her girls.

"So I guess she's the Madame," Cutter whispered. "Maybe she's the woman Amelia said is Thornton's mistress? She is quite attractive."

Harrison shot Cutter a look.

After a long silence, Cutter tried to start a conversation, mostly about his reservations about the entire situation.

"Buddy, have you stopped to really think about what is going on here?" Cutter said.

"What do you mean?" Harrison said.

"Well, I'm just an outside observer, but some of this seems somewhat contrived to me," Cutter said.

There was silence. Cutter finally continued.

"I'm not really sure why you are here, other than to escape from your life for a while," Cutter said. "Don't get me wrong, I totally understand that. But I don't understand why you are so, shall I say, obsessed with this matter. It's not like you really know this woman. She was a friend of your wife's but heck, you had never even met her. And how long were you married?"

Harrison looked at Cutter but then returned his focus to his reconnaissance mission.

"Everyone here seems so tight with each other," Cutter said. "How do you know you're not going to get so entangled into whatever web they've all weaved and then you won't have a way out?"

Harrison still remained silent.

And that's when they heard the gunshot. Both dropped to the ground, attempting to become part of the Earth, and looked to their left, listening for sound and watching for movement. Then they heard the sound of a car engine. They started running in that direction. The same direction where they had hid their own rented vehicle.

"Son of a gun!" Cutter yelled as the vehicle was gone before they reached it. "The chief is not going to be happy about this."

CHAPTER 15

Cutter didn't answer his door when Harrison awoke the next day around lunchtime so he strolled down to Mug's Pub in search of something to fill his empty belly.

When he walked in, Cutter was already full throttle into a hefty roast beef sandwich and was chatting up the piano man. Harrison sat on a bar stool and eyed Cutter inquisitively, who just shrugged and smirked back.

"What'll it be, son, need some hair of the dog that bit 'ya last night?" Frank inquired.

Harrison smiled and said, "No, thanks. Too early for that. How about a cup of that nice coffee and some eggs Benedict? You serve breakfast for lunch?"

"Comin' right up," Frank said as he poured a steamin' cup of coffee and headed for the kitchen. "Lila!"

"So what have you two gentlemen been discussing today?" Harrison inquired, more of Cutter than Woodson.

"Amelia," Woodson said.

Harrison raised an eyebrow as if to say, "Oh?"

"She sent a message. Wants to see you two blokes this afternoon if you can make it over to her school. Said she has something important to tell 'ya."

"Did she say what it's about?" Harrison asked.

"Even if she had told me, I wouldn't violate the lady's trust," Woodson said with a wink.

Harrison knew full well that Woodson knew what was going on. He clearly was ally number two. Harrison had deduced that this Woodson fella somehow knew everything that went on in this town, even though he never seemed to leave the confines of Mug's Pub.

But Harrison didn't press the matter. He would wait to hear whatever was going on firsthand from Amelia.

While Harrison gulped down his eggs Benedict, the restaurant started filling up.

The woman who had been with Thornton on the boat excursion – the one Harrison ran into at the entrance to The Brass Inn – popped in with three other ladies and they sat in a booth. The four women paid no heed to any of the other patrons in the restaurant but greeted Frank warmly as he went over to get his hugs from all of them.

Harrison didn't mention to Cutter that she was the woman he had seen with Thornton, but Cutter knew his partner well enough to know that Harrison had already met this woman at some point just from the way he watched her walk in and sit down, then "surveyed" the situation.

"So did you tell anyone about what happened last night?" Harrison inquired. "You didn't say anything about the car being stolen, did you?"

"Of course not," Cutter said. "Why do you take me for a fool? But I am clearly out of shape. How many miles did we walk?"

"I will take care of the car problem," Harrison said. "Pay the bill and let's get going."

"Oh, I see, I've been sitting here waiting for you to get your ass out of bed all morning and now you're in a hurry," Cutter said. "And have you forgotten who has rank here? Why do I have to pay?"

But the questions fell on deaf ears, as Harrison was already out in front of the establishment hailing a driver to take them to the school. They sat outside for an hour waiting for the young ladies to finish their lessons for the week and be free for the weekend.

"So glad we rushed out of our sanctuary to sit around here," Cutter said.

Some parents had arrived to pick up their daughters to take them home for the two-day break. So Harrison used the opportunity to inquire of some of the parents about the school, how it was run, the lessons the girls learned and the social activities. He was inquiring in part because he was serious about sending Penelope here but also wanted to know if anyone would open up about Thornton or at least release some sort of tidbit.

Harrison learned absolutely nothing. Well, not nothing. He learned that Amelia Adams was the "world's most wonderful teacher, mentor and friend" and that all of her teachers were equally as wonderful. The girls all "adore each of their teachers and their fellow students."

That was a good thing to hear considering he was contemplating sending Penelope here. But it was disconcerting to realize that the parents seemingly were oblivious to the real goings-on at the school.

"Good afternoon, gentlemen," Amelia said. "Care to join me on the porch?"

Warm, not hot, tea arrived along with a plate of delicate pastries. Neither gentleman declined the offerings from the young lady who brought them.

"I see you received my message," Amelia said. "I love Frank and Robert. I can count on them for everything. They do the impossible sometimes."

"They do seem to be on top of almost everything here in town, especially that piano man," Harrison said, trying to hide his sarcasm.

While he appreciated their knowledge of the comings and goings of the townsfolk, he didn't like the idea that they might know Harrison's every move and thought while he was in town.

"Yes, exceedingly knowledgeable," Amelia said, smiling. "I asked you to come here because James was supposed to return yesterday morning and I have not heard hide nor hair of him since he left for his trip Monday morning. I discovered that his mistress was in town the whole time and he wasn't with her."

How Amelia knew this, Cutter and Harrison were afraid to ask.

"When was the last time you heard from him?" Cutter asked instead.

"Monday morning, before he left. Said he would be back by Thursday at 9 a.m. sharp. Claimed he had an important meeting down on Main Street and would stop by the school after he got off the train before he went to his meeting," Amelia said.

"Who was he meeting with?" Harrison asked.

"I don't know, otherwise I would have inquired of whomever that might be to see if he showed up for the appointment," Amelia said. "I checked his schedule that he keeps on his desk but it's blank for the entire month. I assumed it might have had to do with something regarding the town's Board of Trustees. He was appointed to a vacant seat a couple of years ago and spends a lot of time with planning and other dealings."

"Do you know where he went on his trip?" Cutter asked.

"He never divulges such information to me," Amelia said. "Always tells me, 'Don't worry your pretty little head with such details and matters. This is man's work.' And then does whatever he wants with whomever he wants, whenever he wants."

"A real prize of a husband," Cutter mumbled under his breath but loud enough for Harrison to hear.

Harrison shot Cutter a look but Amelia either didn't hear or chose to ignore the comment.

"Do you want us to find him?" Harrison asked. "Or would you prefer he just rode off into the sunset, out of your life and you don't have to worry about him anymore?" Harrison tried to say it light-heartedly and with a smile.

"Unfortunately, while I would like nothing better than to be rid of him forever, I do need your help to at least track him down," Amelia said, then hesitated. "You see, he cleared out all of the bank accounts, or at least the ones he's aware of. I need to at least find my money.

Part of the funds are supposed to go toward my property taxes and to pay for the food service. I also can't let any of the parents or the children or even the townsfolk know what is going on."

Then, the normally poised and stoic Amelia broke down and started sobbing uncontrollably. Harrison reached out to lend a shoulder and his handkerchief.

When she finally was able to control herself again, Harrison said, "We will help you find him and your money. Don't worry about a thing. Just keep things going and don't talk to anyone about this but us, OK? We will take care of this for you. You will not lose your school."

Cutter glanced at him and Harrison offered a meek smile as if to say "I have NO idea how we are going to help her but we will."

Harrison knew Cutter was ready to cut-and-run. But Harrison was determined to figure out a way to help. And deep down, he knew Cutter would remain by his side, even if it meant the wrath of the chief and everyone else, including his wife, who Harrison already knew was not happy that Cutter had taken this "hiatus" to help his buddy on one of his larks.

"Give us the weekend to figure out what we are going to do and let us see if we can find out anything for you," Harrison said. "OK?"

Amelia managed a small smile and a nod of gratitude.

"Now, pull yourself together for the benefit of your girls and don't worry about anything. We will make all of this right. Why don't you meet us on Sunday afternoon for brunch at Mug's Pub, then we'll go take a walk along the river and talk more about this," Harrison said.

Amelia whispered her thanks and said "OK, but I did talk to Robert and Frank about this already."

Harrison said he was not surprised but told her not to tell anyone else.

On the way back in the taxi, Cutter shot Harrison a look.

"Don't even say it," Harrison said. "You know we have to do this and we will figure something out. Just trust me."

"That's what I'm afraid of," Cutter said.

CHAPTER 16

Harrison returned alone to The Brass Inn at 11:30 a.m. on Sunday after taking the train back to Tirtmansic. After meeting with Amelia on Friday afternoon, Harrison and Cutter went home so they could devise a plan. But Harrison also wanted to spend time with Penelope.

Cutter had checked out of his room on Friday because he couldn't stay as long as Harrison and needed to make an appearance back at police headquarters. But Harrison had kept his room over the weekend.

He headed for Mug's Pub at 12:30 p.m. to have lunch with Amelia. Frank noticed Harrison's swagger the moment the front door swung open.

"Where 'ya been, chap?" Frank inquired as Harrison took his top hat off and sat at a table instead of his usual bar stool in the corner.

"What's good today?" Harrison inquired instead.

"Try the roasted chicken with red potatoes and asparagus, I hear they are delish," Frank said. "Gin and tonic?"

Harrison shook his head, "Too early for that. Besides, I'm meeting Amelia. Better stick to a root beer float. Thanks."

Frank chuckled but obliged.

As Frank set the mug full of the root beer float on the table, Harrison noticed the etching on the front of it. "Mug's Pub: Established 1901" On the back it read, "Satisfy your belly with the food and spirits. Satisfy your mind with a new friend."

Harrison had his eye on the door and rose as Amelia entered, focused and smiled. Harrison quickly pulled out Amelia's chair for her.

"Is Mr. Cutter joining us today?" Amelia asked, as she pulled off her white church gloves and bonnet, setting them alongside her Bible on the unoccupied table space beside her.

"I'm afraid he was detained back at home so you're stuck with just me," Harrison smiled.

"I would not use the word 'stuck,' Mr. Harrison. You are quite pleasant company," Amelia said, slightly chastising herself for flirting with her dead friend's husband.

"Anyway, I am sorry that you had to miss church back home to return early today," Amelia continued. "It occurred to me that we could have met later in the day but I did not know how to get word to you back at your residence."

Frank arrived with Amelia's glass of white wine and silently placed it on the table as if he did this every Sunday. Amelia smiled in gratitude.

"Want that gin and tonic now, sir?" Frank asked. Harrison smiled and nodded.

Frank walked away, smiling to himself. The interruption gave Harrison a chance to think of what to say.

"Oh, uh, it was no problem really," Harrison said. "How was your church service?"

"Lovely as always," Amelia said. "I so love our pastor. He always seems to know when I – or anyone in our congregation, for that matter – need to be lifted up to the heavens so that we may again appreciate all that God has given us."

Harrison didn't say anything, thinking about how much God had recently taken away.

"You should come to our service next week if you still are in town, and perhaps bring Penelope so I can meet her and we all can go together," Amelia continued through Harrison's thoughts.

He remained silent.

"You would so enjoy the church and its magical sanctuary," Amelia continued. "I feel so safe inside those humbling walls. And like I said, our pastor is so inspirational. He delivers messages that touch me deep in my heart and soul and helps me forget about the bad of the past week and focus on the good. His words help me start each new week refreshed and ready to impart the lessons to the children."

Harrison still didn't say anything, uncomfortable with the topic of church and God and all things spiritual. He was spiritual, of course, but had been having his own mini debate in his mind ever since this so-called God had so cruelly taken away his one true love, his beloved Madeline, and their daughter Brooke. He had been struggling internally with the issue of God and a higher power and his own spiritual healing ever since.

"How could you take such a beautiful woman away from me, and not even give my beautiful daughter a chance in this world?" he had asked so many times of the air "up there" in the past year.

Many of his and Madeline's friends had tried to convince him that "Madeline's work here was done" or "God needed her and Brooke there." He wasn't buying any of it, at least not right now.

So Harrison changed the subject.

"About the matter at hand," Harrison looked at Amelia inquisitively. "Has your husband resurfaced?"

Just then, Frank arrived to take their order. Amelia said she would have whatever the day's special was, which happened to be the aforementioned chicken meal. Harrison nodded in agreement and said, "Double that."

Frank walked away and then Amelia said, "He has not and I can't say I am disappointed necessarily. I know that is scandalous for a proper wife to say but I am better off without him around. I just wish I knew where my money was. He can go off and never come back as far as I am concerned. I just want my money back so that I can save my school. That dirty scoundrel."

Amelia said that last statement almost to herself.

"Pardon me for the intrusion but I couldn't help overhear that you are wondering where Mr. Thornton might be," Frank interjected as he sat down with his patrons. "Scuttlebutt last night around here was that he, uh, pardon me, ma'am, uh, took off with one of the young ladies from the, uh, well, an establishment called Wild Stallions."

All the while, Frank kept a wary eye on Amelia and her reaction. Harrison also gauged Amelia's reaction and if she had one, she didn't show it.

"Well, I declare, he never was discreet about his visits to his old friend who runs that place," Amelia said. "Good riddance, I say. Oh, but, oh dear. Now what do I do? I need to find my money."

Harrison and Frank both patted Amelia's hands and said they would help her out as best they could.

"I will find your money if it's the last thing I do," Harrison said.

Frank left the table for a minute and returned five minutes later with an envelope and handed it to Amelia.

"What is this?" Amelia asked.

"Open it," Frank said. "But don't be obvious about it."

Amelia nearly fainted when she opened the envelope. It was full of money. An obscene amount of money.

"You found my money?" Amelia said.

"No, no, no," Frank smiled. "I wish I could have done that for you. But we did take up a collection here at the pub. All we had to do was say it was for the school and people chipped in whatever they had in their pockets or pocketbooks. We didn't tell them why, just that it was for you and the young ladies. I wasn't really deceiving anyone. I want you to use it to buy some new textbooks and new teacher's manuals and chalkboards and the chalk and erasers. I know you have old ones and you are OK with that but I want you to get new ones. I know how much you need those things. Nobody in town has to know the real reason. Everyone else in town just thinks it's the right thing to do to help with educating those young ladies."

"I don't know what to say," Amelia said. "Except thank you so much. You have no idea how grateful I am. I don't know how I will ever repay you and the townsfolk for this wonderful gift."

"The only thank you any of us need is to put it to good use, save your school and buy those girls–and yourself–what you need," Frank said.

He then walked away to bring back their lunches and left the duo to eat in peace. Well, except for Robert's piano ramblings. He seemed to be making things up today, Harrison thought.

Harrison was just as stunned as Amelia about the gesture.

"Is that enough to save your school?" Harrison asked.

"I don't know but it's a good start to get the creditors off my back and pay the property taxes," Amelia said.

"Might I offer you some advice? Even if we think he may have left town, we don't know for sure where Thornton is," Harrison said. "Make sure you hide that money in a safe place. I can help you open a new bank account if that would be something that you need."

"Will do," Amelia agreed. "I have my own private bank account that James never knew about. It has a pittance in it but this will help."

Harrison changed the topic again.

"I have a question for you," Harrison said. "You said in your letters to Madeline that you had a couple of allies helping you. Obviously Frank and Robert are assisting you. But the other day you alluded to a third person. Who is that?"

Amelia looked around the room then leaned in and said, "I do have three people helping me. Frank and Robert have been a tremendous help. They're the ones who initially told me about some of the gossip and rumors going around about James and what he was doing to me. He drinks down here quite a bit and that loosens his lips. He's quite talkative with the ladies. He thinks all women are dumb and naïve so has no idea that they are sharing what they learn with Frank and Robert. Robert also has keen hearing so he gets a lot from those conversations. Frank and Robert came to me a year or two ago to tell me what they had been hearing. They weren't sure if it was true or not but it made me do some of my own investigating and it turned out to be true. They also made sure that my letters were sent to

Madeline and I had my mail delivered here. I now have all of the school's mail coming through here."

"Who's the third person helping you?" Harrison asked again.

Amelia seemed reluctant to say, then finally said, "James has a daughter. He doesn't know that I know. He apparently abandoned her before she was even born. Based on information that Frank and Robert were able to glean from some of the patrons here, I happened to find her. She initially was reluctant to help but her desire to get back at what her father did to her and to her mother overwhelmed her to the point that she was willing to do anything possible to see justice brought to the man."

"Where is she now?" Harrison said.

"I don't know," Amelia said. "She was here for a few days last week. She's kind of a wandering soul. I'm trying to get her to come to the school, get some stability in her life and teach her how to read and write. She's a smart kid but she was never given a proper education or even an opportunity, for that matter. Kind of ironic because her father is now president of a school."

"Who is her mother and where is she?" Harrison said.

Amelia suddenly seemed uncomfortable.

"Well, that Wild Stallions place we were talking about earlier? She's the madame. Maggie is her name," Amelia said.

Harrison knew the woman, well, knew of the woman; the buxom red-head. He had only seen her from a distance but knew she was a looker, although he knew that she did not have that same innocent beauty that Amelia and his wife had.

CHAPTER 17

That night, Harrison parked his borrowed car at the edge of the woods a slight distance from the house of entertainment. He donned one of his detective disguises, ditched his duffle bag in the trunk and strolled into Wild Stallions.

The red-headed lady of the house greeted him warmly, saying, "Well, hello big fella, how can I do you tonight?" She laughed boisterously. "Come on in to our parlor and meet some of our other guests. The ladies will be down in a minute. Can I get you a drink?"

It was uncanny to him how much the young lady he had run into twice at the entrance to The Brass Inn, with Thornton on the excursion boat, and now, come to think of it, with Amelia at Mug's Pub on his first day in Tirtmansic, looked just like the woman who obviously was her mother.

When the madame brought his gin and tonic, she sat down on the arm of the chair and leaned her bosom into him. Some of the other girls had come downstairs to join the guests and start their flirtatious games.

"I think I may just have to keep this one for myself," the madame said to only Harrison.

"It's all good, when do we start?" Harrison flirted. "But I think I should know your name first."

"My, my," the madame pretended to be flustered. "Why don't you bring that drink and whatever else you have to show me and follow me."

Harrison dutifully followed the madame up to her luxurious rosy pink boudoire. He had no doubt that the other rooms looked nothing like hers. When they were alone, she finally said, "Name's Maggie" and held out her hand for him to grab and kiss it as most gentlemen did when a lady proffered her hand.

When she started a mini dance routine for him, he pulled out a wad of cash and asked, "How much to just talk?"

She curled her lips in a pout and asked, "Talk?!?!? Are you kidding me? You do know where you are, don't you?"

"I do know where I am, but I need to know something that's more important. And you're the only one who can tell me," Harrison said.

"Oh good God, you're not a cop, are you?" Maggie said. "I thought we had a deal that you people would leave me alone if I didn't cause any problems or disturb the townsfolk."

"Calm down, I'm not here to bust this place up," Harrison said. "James Thornton is a patron of yours. How well do you know him?"

Harrison noted how wide-eyed she became. Then she recovered from her momentary falter and said, "I don't discuss patrons with anyone else. We value their privacy here and I would never violate a patron's trust."

"So you acknowledge he is a customer."

"I did no such thing."

"He was here last Thursday."

Maggie feigned surprise, "So what if he was?"

"He hasn't been seen since," Harrison said.

"And you expect me to know where he is?" Maggie said. "I don't keep tabs on my patrons, except when they are here in my home. Once they leave here, I have no interest in monitoring their actions."

"So how well do you know him?" Harrison said.

"Who?" Maggie asked innocently.

"Don't play games with me or I *will* have you shut down before you can get dressed," Harrison said. "What is your relationship?"

Maggie sighed. She slowly sipped her champagne cocktail while eyeing Harrison.

"How do I know you're not another one of James' associates, here to have your way with me, or worse?" Maggie asked. "You look like you could really harm a lady. That is, if you wanted to. Although . . . I wouldn't have invited you up here if I really thought you were one of his kind."

Harrison silently pondered the "lady" comment. He was curious about her question. Had she experienced horrible things at the hands of one of Thornton's bullies, or Thornton himself? Still, he held his poker face. But there was something about Maggie he liked. Amelia seemed to be empathetic toward her. While he didn't know her, Harrison could see she was a businesswoman first and foremost and he didn't sense the same sense of deceptiveness or callousness that Thornton exuded.

"Look, I'm trying to help a friend," Harrison finally admitted, in the hopes she would open up to him. "I'm not here to question your business practices or your daily operations. I need some information and I think you can help me."

Maggie continued eyeing Harrison suspiciously but something about his aura of kindness touched her heart.

"We had a relationship, an intimate relationship, many years before he married his wife," the madame said. "I guess I probably loved him because I usually avoid having any real relationship with the men who escape to my place. Things became complicated. You see, we have a daughter, but he doesn't care about either one of us. Never has, really. He was just using me and ended our relationship when he found out I was pregnant. He wanted me to take care of it but I couldn't do that. She's basically dead to him anyway. He's never paid any attention to her. He never attempted to pay for anything for her and I told her that her father died years ago."

"Where is she now?" Harrison said.

“She comes and goes,” Maggie said. “I had to make a living for myself and this is all I knew how to do. She was stuck with this as part of her upbringing and I always vowed to get out of the business and give her a respectable living. But this became so lucrative that I just never gave it up. Now that she’s old enough to do what she wants, she does. She still comes back once in a while to visit me, during the days, but I think she just is wandering through life aimlessly now. That’s my only regret, that I could never provide her with a proper education or a proper upbringing. But you do what you have to do.”

“Has she been in town recently?” Harrison asked.

“Um, well, no, I don’t think I’ve seen her in...well, maybe two or three weeks,” Maggie said. “She hung around for a few days and then disappeared again.”

“And you’re sure she doesn’t know that her father is Thornton?” Harrison said.

“Positive. I never told her her father’s name,” the madame said.

CHAPTER 18

So the beautiful young lady Harrison had encountered was indeed Thornton's daughter. And she allegedly was working with Amelia to bring Thornton down. So why was she hanging onto his arm on the excursion boat if she's really helping Amelia? Did Amelia know about this?

Harrison also wondered, "Is she using Thornton, or Amelia? Or both?"

It didn't make sense to Harrison, though. Thornton supposedly had abandoned his daughter before she was even born. Yet he still made appearances at her mother's business so he certainly would have bumped into his daughter on occasion. How had the two made the initial connection? There was no doubt that she was the young woman on Thornton's arm when they encountered each other on the boat.

Did Thornton know that this young woman was his daughter? Did this young woman know that Thornton was her father? Amelia had said that Thornton didn't know that Amelia knew his daughter and Maggie had said she never revealed the father's name to her daughter.

Harrison was perplexed.

"Who's playing who here?" Harrison asked himself.

***

Harrison and Amelia had tea on the porch of one of the buildings at the school on Monday afternoon.

"Do you trust James' daughter, what is her name again?" Harrison asked.

"Emma," Amelia said. "Oh yes, why wouldn't I? She's a doll. She has a good heart, she just needs some guidance. Why?"

"Well, I have discovered that I have run into her on a couple of occasions while I have been here," Harrison said. "She looks just like her mother."

"You've met her mother?" Amelia tried to hide her surprise and seeming disappointment that Harrison apparently had patronized the brothel.

"I just had a conversation with her mother, nothing else," Harrison said, seeing her disapproving look and not knowing why he felt the need to explain himself. "She told me the same thing you told me, that Thornton abandoned her after he found out she was pregnant. She also told me that Emma is wandering aimlessly through life and she regrets not giving her a proper upbringing."

Amelia just nodded sympathetically.

Harrison wondered to himself why Thornton still visited, and was even still welcome, at the brothel, if he had scorned the madame.

"Tell me why you are so interested in taking Emma in under your wing and trust her so much?" Harrison asked. "After all, she is the daughter of a woman who runs a not-so-reputable business. That same woman is the former lover of your husband. Emma could be playing you and working with your husband."

Amelia pondered that for a moment. Then tried to explain.

"My only regret in life is that I happened to meet, fall in love and marry that cad," Amelia said. "I regret that I did not have the smarts to do my own detective work before falling in love with the louse. He preyed on my young, naïve feelings, giving me the attention I was yearning for in my life. And he paid me back by almost destroying everything I have worked so hard to build. My parents had owned all this land and the buildings. After they died, I decided to do something productive with it. This school was my idea, my creation. I had dreamt about this as a little girl.

"Emma is 19 or 20 years old. She needs stability and a focus. She readily agreed to help because her father had never paid attention to her, never helped her get an education yet here he was, the president of a school for young ladies. Why would I not trust her? She and I share a common goal, to bring down that louse and beat him at his own game. You see, the plan is for Emma to reach out to her father after all these years, tell him that she forgives him for abandoning her. He thinks I am dumb and naïve but he also can be dumb and naïve, especially when it comes to the women in his life. Don't underestimate that madame, or me, for that matter. Anyway, Emma is trying to find out what he is up to and what he is using the money, my money, for. We don't have the full plan in place but somehow we are going to extort the money back from him that he was taking from my school. That part was Emma's idea. I'm not so sure I am sold on it. The key is finding out where the money's going."

"No offense but that seems like a really bad idea," Harrison said. "Why haven't you just gone to the Tirtmansic authorities?"

"James is buddies with all of those guys," Amelia said. "They would never listen to me. This is a man's world and they think James is God-like, running this school. I know he's paying them off in some way as well. He's in tight with the police and the government officials. He's told them so many lies that they all think I'm the scoundrel."

CHAPTER 19

Harrison didn't like what he saw. Wild Stallions was abandoned. It was 9 p.m. and there were no lights, no girls and no customers. Harrison approached the house and saw that it was boarded up.

On his way back to town, Harrison went to Mug's Pub. He mentioned to Frank that he had "heard" that Wild Stallions was no longer.

Frank leaned over the bar and said, "Yeah, Robert told me that Thornton was paying off the cops to leave the place alone. But something happened and somehow the cops decided to turn on Maggie. He quit paying the authorities and had the place shut down, I guess. I don't know what happened but people are dropping like flies in this town. I say good riddance to some of them, although, I liked Maggie. Deep down, she's a good woman with a good heart. She just happens to run a small business trying to make a living. Granted, it's not the most reputable way to go about it but who am I to judge?"

"So where did Maggie go? Does anyone know?" Harrison said.

Frank shrugged.

"I'm not sure," Frank said. "But curiously, she stopped in here to give me an envelope full of money to give to Amelia, although she told me not to tell Amelia where it came from. Then Robert said she apparently dropped off a car that someone else had rented, paid the bill and just vanished. Poof. Gone away into the night."

The car that had been stolen from the woods the other night. Which Harrison hadn't reported yet, because he had registered it with a fake name and was wearing a disguise at the time he secured the vehicle.

CHAPTER 20

Amelia's letters to Madeline had detailed the peculiar things that had been going on for the past couple of years. Those details had prompted Harrison to visit Tirtmansic, to investigate Thornton and his financial and governmental dealings. He knew from the letters that Thornton was involved in defrauding the government in his capacity as a public servant. There was something going on with the property taxes but Harrison had not pinpointed what that deception was quite yet.

He also had deduced that Thornton was stealing money outright from the school's coffers and seemingly planned to do something big with the money.

The Tirtmansic officials were either oblivious to his wheelings and dealings, or were a part of the fraud as well. He figured it was the latter because from what Amelia had said, the officials were in lock-step with Thornton. She had written that she was fighting City Hall on several fronts.

Amelia's parents had owned the property where the Annabelle Adams School for Young Ladies now rested. She inherited the property and a nice amount of cash so immediately set out to build a school. The property had been an estate and the buildings were already in existence so it was easy for her to use the funds to renovate the buildings into classrooms and dorm rooms.

During the early 20th Century, property taxes provided upwards of 75 percent of funding for local government services, including for local police, fire, city government, roads, schools and transportation. Amelia's school and a school for boys were the only educational facilities in Tirtmansic. The horse and buggy was the main public transportation but slowly motor vehicles were becoming part of the scenery as well.

Amelia's husband served as president of the school and also was on the Tirtmansic Board of Trustees after being appointed to a vacancy.

Because of his position as president of the school, he abstained from voting on any funding or zoning matters regarding the school and its property, much to his chagrin. However, it didn't prevent him from trying to influence how the others voted. And because he was held in such high esteem among the other elected officials, they usually voted in his favor.

This disgusted Amelia because she was the one who wanted to be on the Board of Trustees. She felt she could bring a much-needed voice of dissent instead of the rubber-stamp it always provided for the people with direct ties to the board members. The board was full of powerful businessmen from the community and women did not have the right to vote let alone serve as an elected official in 1912 America.

Thornton assured her that he would look out for "their" best–and shared–interests.

Still, Amelia couldn't be prevented from speaking out during the public comment session of the meetings. She started creating a lot of noise, attending meetings to make her feelings known about, among other things, how the property tax money was appropriated locally. She told the officials that she was running a school and had been able to do it mostly because she had inherited the property and her family's good name had afforded her the opportunity to secure financial assistance for early operational expenses.

She reminded them that she was the only school in the region for young ladies, teaching them reading, writing and arithmetic, history, politics and science. Her requests to receive some assistance in the form of tax breaks like churches and other entities were receiving, including some of the very politicians she was appealing to, mostly fell on deaf ears.

She finally enlisted the owner of the nearby boys' school to see if working together might help the situation. She even considered some way to start sharing educational opportunities between the schools and maybe establish some well-chaperoned social events between the boys and the girls. She received a welcome response from the owner of the boys' school; they both received cold shoulders from the local politicians, except from her own husband. Or so she thought.

Thornton sat at the meetings pretending to be on her side, supporting her mission of "educating the young ladies to foster their talents and create strong, independent young women who will make a difference in their community and the broader world."

Amelia had been convinced to let him take over the finances of the school so, as he had said, "You can do the real business of educating the girls without having to worry about the business side of things." She had gladly given up that aspect of running the school. But now she learned that he was siphoning off money from the school and hiding it somewhere. For the life of her she could not find where he had buried it.

She had not confronted him yet because she couldn't prove anything. She asked Frank and Robert for their assistance and they gladly jumped in to try and help her solve the mystery of her vanishing funds.

Amelia also suspected something was going on with Thornton as it related to the town's governmental proceedings and other people's businesses as well. Little did she know at the time but he also was messing with agricultural land owners and residential property owners.

The key was to follow the paper trail and see how Thornton was using the money he was stealing.

Amelia discovered that Thornton was charging families a higher tuition than what Amelia established as the tuition years ago–and laundering money through her school from the brothel. He counted on the fact that the families never talked to each other about it and Amelia was too stupid to understand all the creative accounting that he had done with the books.

Thornton simply told Amelia that their revenue couldn't keep up with skyrocketing expenses to keep the school running as a way to cover up what he was stealing.

CHAPTER 21

Amelia told him to lay down on his back on the bed and raise his arms above his head. So long as he did not lower his arms or try to use his hands in anyway, she told him that she would not tie them to the bedposts.

She climbed atop him without actually touching him, her naked body hovering over his naked body. She leaned down and kissed him on the lips. He parted his lips and she slowly slipped her tongue inside his mouth, searching for his. His tongue willingly complied and sought hers. Their tongues explored each other, intertwining with each other and alternating inside his mouth and her mouth.

She pulled away from his mouth with hers and moved over to his ear, tongue lingering, hot and wet, while reaching her hands around to the nape of his neck to caress and massage it.

She moved lower, to kiss and caress his shoulders, then massage his arms and fingers. She sought one of his man nipples with her tongue, circling around it and sucking on it, then sought the other one. She massaged his chest and abdomen while still flicking her tongue on each of his nipples.

She looked up at his face for a reaction and saw his eyes lightly shut with a slight grin of pleasure.

She kept moving down his body with her hands and her mouth, applying light kisses here and there while massaging his hips and reaching for his legs. All the while, she avoided touching in any way his manhood.

She rubbed his right leg, then his left leg, working out all the kinks, stroking up and down. He occasionally propped his head up to watch her and would just smile in acknowledgement of the incredible pleasure she was providing him, then slowly lay his head back down in a state of bliss.

She reached his feet and massaged them, rubbing out all the pain of standing on them all the time. She carefully worked each toe and used her knuckles to rub out the balls of his feet.

She started to massage her way back up each of his legs. Making sure he was still lying back with his eyes closed so he couldn't see what was coming. He briefly opened his eyes and looked down at her, uttering a weak "wow."

The sound of pounding on the door jolted Harrison out of the moment. He stumbled to the door but when he opened it, nobody was there. He ran his fingers through his hair and shook the not-so-proper thoughts of his wife's friend out of his mind.

He looked out his hotel window down onto Main Street. There had been a downpour but now, at dusk, the sun was casting a late afternoon, early evening glow.

Harrison thought he saw something strange in the cobblestones. With the way the sun was hitting the wet bricks, there was a clear difference in how the cracks were formed and the way the bricks were haphazardly aligned in one area. It was a contrast to the perfection displayed on the rest of the street.

"Kudos to the bricklayer," Harrison muttered about the seeming flawlessness.

But if the bricklayer had been such a perfectionist, why was one area so misshapen?

Harrison waited for the darkness to find out, after everyone had gone home to their families or other pursuits for the evening. Then he descended onto the relatively dark Main Street to check out the cobblestones up close and personal.

His right heel started clicking the moment he stepped on the cobblestones.

"Hush," he whispered, as if the nail was an animate object.

He used his lighting device to examine the deformed cobblestones and then started feeling around. He quickly discovered that he was able to pull a section of the cobblestones up, almost like a doorway had been cut into the street. He looked around but saw no one in the vicinity.

After laboring a bit to raise the door, he peered inside with his light. He climbed down the makeshift steps and quietly shut the makeshift door. It had a locking mechanism on the inside but nobody had locked it. At the bottom of the rungs, he discovered what seemed like an intricate set of tunnels. They darted off in four different directions.

Harrison wandered a bit to get a sense of the layout but decided to wait for Cutter to do a real excursion. This was one of those situations where it was better to bring not only the proper equipment but also a partner.

As he started to climb back up the makeshift steps that would lead him back out onto the street, something caught his right sleeve. He felt around with his free hand and then pulled at the contraption in the dark. Then he shone his light. It wasn't in his personality to let much shock him but this wasn't at all what he expected to encounter.

Harrison closed the secret compartment, then locked the door leading out onto Main Street, just in case someone else decided to try to descend into the maze of tunnels from that route. He climbed back down the steps and followed the tunnels to the east in search of another exit. One tunnel led him directly to the basement of The Brass Inn.

Harrison returned to his room, pulled his journal out of hiding and noted what he had found. He also flipped through the letters that Madeline and Amelia had exchanged over the years. He had read them seemingly a hundred times and still kept searching for clues.

He made a notation to see if he could get access to Robert Woodson's journals of the town's coming and goings, or at least a chance to debrief Woodson on what he knew.

Then he closed the journal and wrote a letter to his daughter.

My Dearest Sweet Pea,

I hope you know how much Daddy loves you. You have given me a reason to live and go on pursuing justice. I always have wanted to make the world a better place for your Mommy and now for you. You know how much your Mommy and I loved you, even before you arrived on that glorious day to meet us?

I want to be there to take care of you every day of your life. I want to read to you every night, tuck you in and watch you sleep so peacefully. I enjoy that sacred time that only you and I share each night and I am sorry I have not been there these past couple of weeks to do that. But I will be back soon.

The most important thing is for you to stay safe. I sometimes forget that I have a responsibility to stay safe for you. If it was just me, I would not be as concerned about my own safety. But you are a constant reminder that I need to be cautious and make sure I return to you, especially now that I am your sole parent and provider. Thoughts of you remind me daily to watch out for the bad guys.

I can't wait to see you grow up into as fine a young lady as your mother was, although I am not looking forward to the boys who most assuredly will come calling to take you out on dates. How about we agree that you can go on dates when you are about 30 years old?

I look forward to the day that I walk you down the aisle to your own husband with bittersweet feelings. I know I will be losing my little girl to another man but I know that you and I will always have that special father-daughter bond that can never be broken. I also so want you to find the kind of unconditional, crazy and beautiful love that your mother and I shared. That love created you and your sister Brooke.

Always remember how proud your mother and I are of you and know how much we love and adore our little Sweet Pea.

With love always,

Your father

The next day, Harrison dropped the letter to his daughter at the clerk's desk and asked if he could post it for him.

Harrison also called Cutter and asked him to return.

"I've discovered something that you need to help me with," Harrison said. "We're going to need to get the local authorities involved at some point, I'm afraid, but I want you in on this to help me wrap up the case before I go to them. When can you get here? The sooner, the better."

Cutter said he would do his best to get back to town but "The chief's being his difficult self right now. Can you tell me anything now?"

"No, you need to be here in Tirtmansic," Harrison insisted. "I found something and I need you to bring our night gear, some lights and some evidence bags. Big ones."

Harrison paused, then added one of his usual ribbings for good measure, "Oh, and could you manage to pack your courage as well?"

"Humorous. I'll be there by Saturday," Cutter said. "Try not to get yourself killed by then."

When Harrison hung up, there was an urgent knock at his hotel door.

"Just a minute," Harrison said, and hastily packed away his journal and the letters in their secret place.

When he opened the door, he was stunned to see who stood opposite him.

CHAPTER 22

The street was deserted and dark but I did not feel alone in his presence. He filled the emptiness of the quieted street. We lingered, pretending to look at the items in the darkened, angled entrance-way to the closed store. The windows showcased an elegant, all-white baby crib, an old-time bouncing pony and baby clothes. Ironic, as both of were mindful of ensuring that no baby would be conceived.

As I grew bored, and turned to walk away, he grabbed my left buttock and swung me around to face him in one swift movement. He still held my left buttock as he wrapped his other arm around my waist and pulled me close enough to feel his desire. He stared into my eyes and communicated what his mouth wanted to do just before he plunged his wet, sweet, minty tongue into my waiting, wet mouth.

He was drunk with alcohol, I was drunk with the headiness of his embrace, his caress on the hollow of my back. He slipped his tongue in and out, exploring my mouth with abandoned passion. My tongue greeted his, each trying to out-do the other, explore more, faster and without reservation. Our bodies began a slow, seductive dance, in sync with each other's movement, rocking as our kiss grew deeper, hotter, wetter. It was just a kiss, but, oh, what a kiss it was.

Then he abruptly let go, coming to his senses, saying we both must part and go our separate ways. I could hear the longing in his voice, in his lingering touch and his pleading eyes.

I wanted to stay in that moment, but knew we must leave. Alone.

Amelia woke with a start and felt the flush of her blushing face. She had to regain her senses. "Did Harrison and I actually do that? Or was I just dreaming?"

Amelia could not remember what had happened last night. Whether it was real or imagined, Amelia knew she could not have such thoughts about her best friend's – deceased or not – husband.

Amelia wandered to the kitchen to start the hot water for her tea. As she gazed out, she thought she saw a figure darting from one tree to another. The person was too far away to see if it was male or female. She shook it off as just the girls playing around the grounds of the school before morning lessons.

Still, she rang Robert to see if he could come out and check the grounds for anything out of the ordinary.

CHAPTER 23

Cutter returned Saturday but Harrison didn't meet him at the train station, which he thought was peculiar. Yet Cutter wasn't worried. Harrison was a little absent-minded sometimes, especially when he became entrenched in an investigation.

"I'm pretty easy to forget," Cutter chuckled to himself in his self-deprecating way.

Cutter hailed a taxi to The Brass Inn, checked in and dumped his gear in his room. He then knocked on Room 212. No answer. It was almost lunchtime so Cutter headed to Mug's Pub, thinking Harrison might be indulging. Cutter thought he could use a bite to eat as well. He never was comfortable trying to eat on a moving locomotive.

When his eyes had adjusted to the darkness within Mug's, he did not see Harrison. If he was there, Cutter knew Harrison would be sitting somewhere with his back to the wall, facing the entrance. He took a seat on a bar stool and inquired of Frank as to where he might find Harrison.

Frank shrugged and said, "I don't know. Haven't seen him in a few days. Figured he might have gone home to spend time with his daughter."

Cutter ate a quick lunch and then tried to hail another taxi to the young ladies' school.

"Miss Amelia isn't there today, Mr. Cutter," said the taxi driver, the same one who had driven Harrison and Cutter to the school the first time Cutter was in town.

"Where is she?" Cutter asked.

"Having lunch with her lady friends at the Tilted Tea Pot. That's where they go every Saturday afternoon," the driver told him.

"Ah," Cutter said. "Say, you wouldn't happen to know where my partner, Harrison, is, would you? Frank said he hadn't seen him for a couple of days."

"Can't say I do, sir," the driver said. "Haven't seen him myself in a couple of days, either, now that you mention it."

Cutter thanked the driver and walked south on Main Street toward The Tilted Teapot. He hung around on one of the benches across the street until he saw the women emerge from the restaurant.

He walked across the street and Amelia's eyes lit up as she smiled in recognition of Cutter. She separated herself from the other ladies and greeted him warmly.

"How are you this fine day, Mr. Cutter?"

"Good, my dear lady, and how are you?"

"Good, good. I hope everything is OK?" Amelia asked inquisitively.

"Why wouldn't it be?" Cutter said.

Amelia grabbed Cutter's elbow and turned him away so the ladies couldn't hear them.

"Honestly, I'm not sure," Amelia said. "I thought that Harrison was going to meet me this morning. He said he had some important news to share. He never showed and I haven't seen him in a couple of days. Then you show up here, waiting for me. I assumed the worst."

"To be honest, I don't know where he is, either," Cutter said. "He summoned me a few days ago but today was the earliest I could get here. I knocked at his room and he didn't answer. I went to Mug's Pub and Frank said he hasn't seen him in a couple of days. I was hoping you knew where he was or that he might be with you."

Now Cutter was beginning to worry, but tried not to let Amelia know that.

"I am sure he is somewhere doing something with the investigation," Cutter said. "Don't worry about it. Why don't you return to your afternoon with the ladies and he and I will be in touch when I hook up with him?"

Amelia smiled uneasily but agreed and the two parted ways. Cutter headed back to The Brass Inn and inquired of the desk clerk as to when he had last seen Harrison. The clerk said he was the weekend clerk so had not seen him since last Sunday, when he arrived back in town.

"I can inquire of the chambermaids as to the last time they made up the room," the clerk offered. "Mr. Parker had told us that it wasn't necessary to make up the room every day and that he would let the clerk know when he needed fresh towels and bed sheets. I can find out when he did that last."

The clerk checked the log and then dialed the rotary phone on his desk to ring up housekeeping.

"It appears they last were in his room on Thursday," the clerk said.

Cutter's bad feeling returned.

"Is the owner around? I would like to enter his room and see if he left a trace of where he might have gone?" Cutter said, flashing his police badge.

The clerk departed and returned with a grim-looking man.

"John Ryan, I am the hotel keeper," the man said, offering his hand to Cutter. "Might I inquire as to why you need to enter another patron's room?"

Cutter flashed his badge again and said, "I am a police detective and the gentleman in room 212 is my partner, also a detective. From what I have been able to surmise, he has not been seen in at least two days. I am working on something with him and need to see if he left a clue as to where he might be."

Ryan studied Cutter's badge for a while.

"Why are you and your partner in Tirtmansic?" Ryan asked.

"My partner is here on a personal matter that required a little bit of unofficial detective work," Cutter said. "I simply am back-up."

Ryan scrutinized the man and finally sighed.

"Very well, then," Ryan said. "Follow me."

Cutter followed the man up the velvet-lined steps and Mr. Ryan unlocked the door to room 212.

Cutter caught a glimpse of blood before Ryan had the door fully open. Then John Ryan gasped and exclaimed "OH DEAR LORD! Call the police!"

Cutter caught the irony in the statement, as he was the police. But he knew what this chap meant.

CHAPTER 24

"Death by gunshot wound to the chest" was the official ruling from the Tirtmansic coroner.

His own police chief was not pleased when Cutter relayed the news of Harrison's death. He was livid that Cutter had allowed Harrison to go on a fishing expedition of a personal nature that was not official police business.

"Det. Parker claimed it was official business related to a case he was working on here!" the chief yelled into the phone. "What was this nonsense about a mystery involving his wife's friend and why in the hell did you allow him to get mixed up in whatever this is??!?!!?"

Cutter wondered why he was the one in trouble when Harrison was the one who concocted the cover story for his excursion. Aside from the fact that Harrison was now dead so the chief couldn't yell at him. But that was beside the point. The chief seemed to be even more upset that Cutter had run interference and covered up for his partner.

"YOU should know better!" the chief had yelled into the phone when Cutter fessed up to the truth. "I am holding you personally responsible for the death of one of our best detectives. One more screw-up, Cutter, and you'll be doing patrol duty on the back of a horse! You hear me? We'll talk about this when you get your ass back here to headquarters. And it better be pronto!"

Cutter didn't answer the chief, just listened to him rant.

"Like I had any control over anything Harrison did anyway," Cutter thought to himself. "He's always been a maverick. And this involved someone from his wife's past. I wouldn't have even attempted to talk him out of this."

Cutter didn't mention the fact that the chief was the one who approved the excursion.

Cutter had no intention of heading back home "pronto!" He planned to stay right here to work with the local authorities to try and piece together what had happened to his buddy. Then he would accompany Harrison's body back for a proper police burial. Which reminded him: Penelope. Suddenly Cutter remembered that beautiful girl who now had lost her father, too.

Cutter thought he should be the one to tell her grandparents and would offer to tell Penelope with them.

"How am I ever going to do that?" Cutter asked himself.

His thoughts were interrupted when he heard the phone slam down on the other end. He hadn't even heard the end of the conversation.

Cutter had been sitting in Tirtmansic's meager police station, situated on the southernmost end of Main Street. Everyone heard the conversation. Some nodded at him knowingly while others tried to avoid looking directly at him. He soon found out why.

George Greyber, the big-boned, heavy-set Tirtmansic Police Chief, called him into his office for a chat.

"Sgt. Cutter, you're a smart chap, right?" the chief asked, rhetorically.

Cutter got a bad feeling in his already twisted gut. He just nodded.

"What in the hell are you and your partner doing snooping around my town and what the hell are you investigating that the local authorities should be investigating, if in fact there is anything to investigate?" Greyber yelled.

"Sir, no disrespect meant," Cutter said. "My partner was simply here on an investigation of a personal matter. He was here assisting a friend of his deceased wife's. There was nothing sinister about it."

Cutter knew he could weasel his way out of this chief's office because his own chief would never admit that "his boys" were conducting "official business" on someone else's territory without his knowledge or approval. Cutter also didn't want to reveal the exact truth because, quite frankly, he didn't even know the full story. That had died with Harrison.

Cutter also knew that the police chief and some of his underlings were thick into the schemes that involved Thornton.

"Then why is he dead?" Greyber boomed.

"I would like to know the answer to that question as well," Cutter said. "If you would be so kind as to let me continue working with your men on the official investigation, and have access to all of the forensics, I can assure you that we all can find out the answer to that question together."

"Like hell I will let you, a foreigner, inject yourself into my investigation," Greyber boomed louder. "You have no right to be here and no interest whatsoever in this investigation. My men are highly-trained and qualified to handle this on their own."

Cutter was about to respond that he did have an interest in the matter when one of Tirtmansic's police sergeants knocked, poked his head in and said, "Uh, chief, I'm directing the investigation and I am OK if Sgt. Cutter here would like to help us. If nothing else, he can give us a profile on his partner and maybe help us figure out what he was doing and how he got tangled up with the wrong person."

The chief, who must have had a tremendous amount of respect for this particular sergeant – that, or the sergeant had something on the chief – finally relented and nodded his approval.

Cutter took that as his sign to get the heck out of the office and start working with the much friendlier sergeant.

CHAPTER 25

Still, Cutter was reluctant to pursue the case after Harrison's death. Well, that is not the total truth. In reality, Cutter was neutered in the matter, by the local authorities and his own chief.

"You were right all along," Cutter had told Amelia after Harrison's death. "Thornton, your husband, ma'am, is chummy with the local authorities. Any accusations of fraud, allegations of corruption or anything else against him has been covered up or will be covered up because he controls the purse strings. He used his role on the Tirtmansic Board of Trustees and also unofficially. He wielded his power and influence over the chief and his minions by lining their pockets with a little extra cash. I guess he was giving out bonuses."

"How do you know this for certain?" Amelia asked.

"Harrison and I had found out that much together," Cutter said. "The plan was for me to come back here to Tirtmansic, Harrison would brief me on whatever else he had discovered on his own, and then the two of us were going to share it all with you. Unfortunately, I never got the chance to hear about his discoveries but I know it was something big because he asked me to bring our evidence-gathering equipment. And he insisted I return right away because it couldn't wait. But I had pressing matters back home that detained me."

"We hadn't determined who to turn to, someone with a position of authority, to turn your husband in along with the rest who were receiving kickbacks," Cutter continued. "We knew we couldn't come out and start accusing the locals because we would be the know-nothing out-of-towners, in their view. But we were going to gather the irrefutable evidence and present it to the proper authorities."

"So they all just get away with it now?" Amelia asked.

"Not necessarily, ma'am," Cutter said. "I have seen the Tirtmansic officials, especially the police department, firsthand and they need someone to rat them out. So I made the decision to call in the state police agency to investigate. Harrison and I had discussed it as an option and since I can't bring him back or investigate what happened to him, I can make sure that these corrupt officials are halted."

Unfortunately, while the state police did investigate and confirm the theories of corruption at all levels of the local government, the state police did little but outline a plan of action to implement some better controls and policies for the future.

Cutter learned that their feeling was that Thornton was gone, the issue was a moot point. If Thornton turned up again, they might want to consider charges against him. But the guilty party was gone and the state police didn't make much effort to try and prosecute some of the officers who were directly involved in the kickback schemes either.

"The lack of a paper trail because it all was done with cash doesn't give us enough evidence to take it to a jury," a state prosecutor told Cutter. "Without Thornton, we don't know for sure who received the kickbacks. And truth be told, the state doesn't want to go to the expense and embarrassment of a high-profile trial involving those who were entrusted to protect and serve. It could put an unnecessary target on the backs of the innocents–like you, sir—when people start associating the few corrupt police officers with all of them."

The state agency also concluded that it was more of a local matter and that the fine folks of Tirtmansic could handle the situation by electing honorable officials and cleaning house on the bureaucratic level.

Cutter took that to mean that the state police didn't want to have to investigate their own.

Meanwhile, Cutter grieved. He felt incredible remorse, regret and most of all, guilt about Harrison's death. He and Harrison had always had a fondness for their alcohol, but after Harrison's death, the bottle became Cutter's new buddy. His real buddy was gone and there was never going to be anyone who could replace him.

The local authorities termed Harrison's death an "accidental gunshot wound," out of respect for the family. They unofficially told Cutter they believed Harrison had committed suicide. They had learned during the interview of Harrison's in-laws that Harrison had been despondent over the loss of his wife and had even acknowledged that he wasn't being much of a father to his daughter. That was the explanation for Penelope living with her grandparents for the past year. And he had wandered away for a few weeks to take care of other matters, "meaning, he needed to leave town to kill himself."

"But he never would have killed himself," Cutter had pleaded with the Tirtmansic police chief and his underlings and the mayor and anyone else who would listen to him. "It's impossible. The thought would have never crossed his mind and I know him. He always was careful with his weapons. This was no accident. He never would have left his beloved Penelope to be an orphan. It's just not true."

Cutter's arguments and protests and outbursts fell on deaf ears. The only ones who seemed to listen to him were Frank and Robert. They also had become fond of Harrison during his time in town and wanted to see justice served.

Yet, to the local authorities, it made perfect sense that Det. Harrison Parker would head to a strange town to get away from all the reminders back home. The locals had reported seeing Harrison imbibe quite a bit of alcohol in his frequent visits to Mug's Pub. The official conclusion was that he already was slowly drinking himself to death.

"He had too much to drink the night of his death and accidentally shot himself. Case closed," Greyber, the Tirtmansic police chief, said to Cutter as he closed the folder to emphasize his point.

Cutter wasn't buying the story and never would. He saw the crime scene, albeit briefly and with a heavy escort of the locals. But in his mind, there was no way Harrison had accidentally shot himself.

Harrison's in-laws also were astonished to learn from Cutter that their words from the police interview had been twisted around.

"Yes, we verified that Harrison was a despondent widower and we were helping him raise his daughter, offering our full love and support to both of them," Madeline's mother had told Cutter. "We have known this kind, gentle man for years and he would never harm himself. He wouldn't harm a soul unless his wife or daughter's life was threatened. And he might defend himself if his own life was threatened. But he would never try to kill himself or drink himself to death. He would never, ever do that to his daughter."

Harrison's in-laws said they had known he was on a mission to investigate something. But they had seen how much pain he had been in after Madeline's death and knew that he knew how much pain it had caused his daughter.

"He would never willingly put his daughter through that again," they told Cutter.

Cutter's feelings on the matter echoed their sentiments. He knew Harrison loved his daughter way too much to leave her as an orphan. He pressed the matter for some time but grew weary when he kept hitting brick walls, and his own chief threatened to fire him if he didn't back off.

Cutter realized that even though it was a police officer who had been killed, it wasn't one of "the local" cops so the Tirtmansic police did a shabby job of investigating the case in his opinion. Cutter learned that their evidence-gathering skills either were sorely lacking and in need of major revamping, or they simply had no idea how to run a murder investigation. As it turns out, they never had to. His own chief didn't give him much support in trying to track down the killer and eventually ordered him to return to his real job, protecting the fine citizens of his own town, and to leave the citizens of Tirtmansic in the "capable" hands of the Tirtmansic Police Department.

Cutter was miserable without his partner around and felt responsible for Harrison's death, even though he knew he could never stop Harrison from pursuing this case. When Harrison was hell-bent on pursuing something, Cutter knew he was a lost cause. So he learned to either keep his mouth shut and not get involved, or join him. The majority of the time, he just joined Harrison, sometimes reluctantly and begrudgingly.

Cutter became paralyzed from the incident and couldn't muster the ability to go out and investigate much of anything on his own after that.

He knew that if Harrison was the one still here and Cutter had died that Harrison would be able to carry on, and probably with more of a vengeance than ever. But Cutter admitted willingly that he was never as strong as Harrison, and was weakened even more with his partner gone. His demons paralyzed him while Harrison's demons had motivated him.

CHAPTER 26

Amelia and Emma had started an unlikely friendship about a year before Detective Harrison and his sidekick arrived in Tirtmansic. Amelia had noticed the young lady sitting by herself at the bar one day when she was eating lunch at Mug's Pub. She inquired of Robert as to who the young lady might be.

"She seems somewhat lost and forlorn," Amelia had said.

Robert, who knew everyone, shrugged and said, "First time she's been in here. I don't know yet."

Amelia had no doubt he would know her full story in no time. In the meantime, Amelia decided to take a seat at the bar next to her. Frank came over to take her order and then Amelia sized up her neighbor.

"You wouldn't happen to be the young lady I'm supposed to meet about the teaching position, would you?" Amelia asked the young lady, who gave her a perplexed look.

"I don't think so," Emma said, focusing on the half-empty plate of roasted beef stew in front of her.

"Oh, that's a shame," Amelia said. "I'm Amelia. I own a school for young ladies and I really could use some help with the girls. You wouldn't happen to know if another lady was in here looking for me?"

Emma shook her head no.

"How about you?" Amelia said. "It may be presumptuous of me but what kind of background do you have? Would you be interested in teaching some young girls a thing or two about life?"

"I don't think you'd want me to be teaching your proper young ladies anything," Emma said. "I don't know nothing about no education stuff. I haven't been in a classroom since I was little. I learned everything I need to know on the streets and by observing the life around me."

Amelia refrained from correcting the girl's English and pondered a new approach.

"I have an idea," Amelia said. "Why don't you come to my school tomorrow? I'll give you directions or I can arrange for a driver to come get you at your home. You're a little older than most of the girls at the school but I could teach you one-on-one, giving you the basics of reading and writing and arithmetic. Then once you are comfortable enough with the material, I will make you my assistant and you can help me teach the other girls."

Emma didn't respond, just kept contemplating the food on her plate. Her fork clanked on the side of the plate and she turned to study Amelia.

"What do you want from me?" Emma asked abruptly.

Amelia was taken aback but continued to smile and said, "I just want to help you get an education and provide an opportunity for you. Forgive me for being so blunt but I am guessing that you could use a friend and I could be your mentor and friend and teach you the finer things of being a lady."

Emma looked at her suspiciously.

"I don't need no help from anyone. I do fine by myself," Emma retorted.

"I don't need help from anyone," Amelia corrected.

"That's what I said," Emma said.

"I meant that proper English would be 'I don't need help from anyone,' not 'I don't need no help from anyone'," Amelia said. "You don't need the word 'no' in the sentence because it creates a double negative."

Emma looked even more bewildered.

"Never you mind for the moment," Amelia said. "Just come to my school tomorrow morning, I will show you around and we can work on refining your skills."

Amelia asked Frank for a pen and paper and wrote out her name, the name of the school and directions from Main Street.

"Here are the directions from here, or would you like for me to send a driver to pick you up at your home?" Amelia asked.

"I'll find my way," Emma said.

"Great. I look forward to it," Amelia said. "I'm Amelia. What did you say your name is?"

"I didn't," Emma said.

Amelia smiled patiently. Amelia still didn't say anything and when her food arrived, she just started eating.

"Emma," the girl said. "Just Emma. Please don't ask me anymore questions."

Amelia made a note to work on the girl's manners in polite company. But she refrained from correcting her in this setting.

***

Emma did not show up the next day. Amelia was disappointed but not surprised.

Amelia didn't know where Emma found her shelter each night and didn't know who her parents were. But Amelia had the feeling that Emma needed someone to support and encourage her.

A few weeks after her initial encounter with Emma, Amelia sat with Robert Woodson for a late lunch at Mug's Pub. True to his form, Robert had ferreted out some information from the young girl.

"You are a genius," Amelia said. "That personality of yours could win over anyone. So what did she say?"

The duo was sitting in the back booth and Robert lowered his voice.

"She's your husband's daughter," Robert said.

Amelia nearly choked on her squash.

"Say that again," Amelia said.

Robert winked and said, "You heard me."

"How is that possible?" Amelia asked.

Robert leaned in closer.

"Well, there's no delicate way to say this but here goes," Robert said. "Her mother is Maggie, the beautiful madame who runs Wild Stallions. Forgive me, m'lady."

Amelia sat in stunned silence.

"I had a couple of drinks with Emma the other night when the place was empty," Robert went on. "She told Frank and I about her desolate and desperate formative years, years in which she basically was left to fend for herself. Her mother runs Wild Stallions but doesn't own it. It appears that one James Thornton, your husband, ma'am, I'm afraid is the silent owner. Her mother, Maggie, never told her or acknowledged that James was her father. But somehow Emma had figured it out."

"How?" Amelia asked, trying to recover. Nothing James did now or in the past surprised her anymore by this point.

"I have no concrete proof but I definitely see a connection between my mother and father whenever he comes around," Emma had told Robert and Frank. "My mother always gets this odd distant look in her eyes and becomes despondent for a couple of days after he visits."

Emma had told the men that the pattern seemed to be that her father came around only when he needed something.

"He pays absolutely no attention to me but I'm not sure he knows who I am or what I'm doing there," Emma had told them, Robert said in relating the prior conversation. "I usually am banished to the kitchen or running an errand when he shows up. But you can learn a lot by hiding in the shadows and listening to people's conversations. I also found my Mom's old scrapbooks and photo albums. There is no father listed on my birth certificate, but there are photos of my mother with James Thornton leading up to when my mother would have been pregnant."

Later, when Amelia confronted Emma about what Robert had told her, Emma confirmed it.

"And let me tell you something," Emma told Amelia. "That man you are married to, my father, is a no-good scumbag. Excuse me for not being a lady but it's the truth. You would be better off without him."

Amelia already knew this to be fact but at first, didn't share anything with Emma about what he was up to. This revelation presented a new set of challenges for Amelia. She had offered to school the girl and the offer remained open. Thornton didn't know – or pretended not to know – that Emma was his daughter. But Emma knew and what would happen if she confronted Thornton about it?

That was the least of her concerns, though. Amelia needed to free herself of James but she didn't know how. Women didn't get a divorce from their husbands in 1911 America.

She enlisted Frank and Robert's help once again and had them be intermediaries between herself and Emma.

"You two seem to connect with her on a level that I can't," Amelia had told them.

"Well, of course, m'lady," Robert had said. He and Frank exchanged some kind of knowing glance that clearly indicated that Amelia was the outsider on this matter.

"We have the charms of the gentleman's species," Robert said. "She likes the attention of gentlemen. You have nothing to offer her in that department."

Amelia wasn't offended.

"You boys are dreaming. You two are old enough to be her father," Amelia said. They all chuckled.

Amelia and Emma got to know each other a little bit better, and then one night, the group of Frank, Robert, Amelia and Emma concocted a plan.

"Why not let your father know that he has a daughter and tell him that you want to get to know him better?" Robert asked.

Amelia, who had had three glasses of wine, two more than her personal limit, rolled her eyes.

"That has to be the dumbest idea you've had...today," Amelia said, and giggled.

"No, seriously, listen," Robert said. "He doesn't know that you and Emma know each other and that Emma is his daughter. She suddenly appears and pretends to be just like him, a little sly fox who wants in on whatever scheme he's playing. Of course, we don't quite know what that is yet but I have faith that Emma can work some womanly magic. She has the motivation to do it, too. Let her bring him into her world, leak a few 'details' about the way her mother runs her business, maybe even make some well-placed, um, uh, not so flattering comments about your school, and maybe even about you to make it more believable to him. Once he has seen that his beautiful daughter is just like him, he might trust her enough to bring her in on his plans."

The others contemplated the concept.

"Emma has a couple of cute girlfriends, I've seen you with them," Robert said, winking at Emma. "We can add a little bit of spice to the equation by having them come around when you're around. He'll be wanting to meet you all the time just so he can flirt with your friends."

"I don't like the idea of using Emma and her friends to get the goods on James," Amelia said. "This is my problem, not theirs."

"I don't mind," Emma said. "And my friends love to mess with men's minds. I don't need to tell them what we're up to, just let them know that there's this guy who needs to be messed with and he'll buy us some drinks, we'll have a few laughs and be done with it."

Amelia stared at Emma.

"You don't know what this man is like, Emma," Amelia said. "He's not someone you mess with and expect to come away on top. He is the master of manipulating people and he can see right through anyone who's trying to pull a fast one on him. He will get revenge on you and you won't even see it coming. I won't let you be part of that."

"You don't have a say in what I choose to do or not do," Emma said. "I'm a grown woman, I can take care of myself. You need to save your school and rid my evil father from your life. I don't know what you've done so far to try to get rid of him but whatever it is, it's not working, right?"

Amelia had to nod in agreement.

Then Emma looked at Robert.

"I'm all in," Emma said. "When do the games begin?"

CHAPTER 27

Emma went to the school a couple of days later and asked to see the president. He was unavailable, his secretary told her.

"I think he's going to want to see me," Emma said firmly but with a smile. "Tell him his daughter wants to speak with him. Now!"

The secretary rushed into the boss' office and spoke quietly to him. She came to the door and motioned for Emma to enter, "He'll see you right now, ma'am."

Emma already disliked the man but his slimy fake smile when he saw her made her stomach churn.

"Well, Miss Emma, isn't it?" Thornton said. "Please, do, come on in and rest and have a seat on one of my plush sofas. Can I have Ruth get you something to drink?"

"No thank you," Emma said and smiled politely at the secretary as she closed the door. Emma knew Ruth was already spreading the news around campus that Thornton had a visitor claiming to be his daughter.

"Now, what was that silly little fib you told my secretary so you could have a private word with me?" Thornton said, with a fake smile.

"It wasn't a 'silly little fib,' as you call it," Emma said stone-faced. "It's the truth. I'm your daughter."

"Now, I'm not sure where you mustered up this little fantasy of yours but that's not possible," Thornton said, the smile fading, replaced with worry lines.

"Did you or did you not have a love affair with my mother, Maggie, who runs your little business known as Wild Stallions, say about 21 years ago?" Emma asked point blank.

Sweat beads started forming on Thornton's shiny head. The smile was completely eradicated.

"My mother's never told me who my father was," Emma said. "She said she was protecting me from the, and I use her word, 'scoundrel,' who may have impregnated her but certainly was not daddy material. Over the years, I never questioned her but then I started noticing how you two interact whenever you come around. And she gets so despondent and upset. I put it together."

"You listen here, little missy," Thornton said. "If this is true, you are to utter this to no one. I am the president of this school for young ladies and I am a member of the Tirtmansic Board of Trustees. I have a reputation to uphold and I will not have the people of this town muttering behind my back that I fathered a child with a whore."

The comment stung Emma. She wasn't always close to her mother but she was protective of her and hated her mother's reputation. Her mother didn't entertain any of the customers, just her own gentleman who wasn't really a customer. She let the rest of the women who worked for her do most of the entertaining. Emma wrestled with the concept that while her mother wasn't directly involved in the transactions, she did provide a venue and placed other women in a position of having a not-so-glowing reputation. So technically, wasn't her mother perpetuating the problem?

Still, Emma kept her composure and didn't let Thornton know how much the comment hurt.

"I'll keep it our little secret for now," Emma said. "I won't even tell Mother that I know who my father is. But you are going to do some things for me."

"I don't think you're in a position to be making demands, young lady," Thornton said.

"I think I am and I will," Emma retorted. "Here's the situation. I know you are up to something with this school and with the town's officials. I want in on it, a share of whatever financial scheme you're playing."

Thornton's entire bald head and face had turned bright red.

"I don't know what you're talking about," Thornton said.

"I know what kind of mischief and mayhem you're into because I have friends in well-placed positions," Emma said. "I don't know all the details but you are going to tell me and bring me in as a partner."

"I will do no such thing," Thornton said.

"You will, because otherwise, I go to your precious young wife, that Amelia lady, and tell her everything," Emma said with a stoic smile.

She thought he might pass out. He got up and poured himself a bourbon from the glass tea cart at the far end of the office. When he turned around, she saw that the large glass was full. He took a swig and just as fast, the glass was only a quarter full.

Thornton came back over to her, walking slowly, obviously pondering his next words carefully.

"How much do you know?" Thornton asked.

"I will not reveal all of that right now," Emma said.

She stood and moved toward the door, suddenly fearing being alone in the office with this big man who had just chugged a significant amount of liquor. "Meet me at Mug's Pub tomorrow night promptly at 7 p.m. and we will discuss the details further. Be prepared to tell me everything and then we will work out the arrangements of this new little father-daughter venture."

Emma grabbed the door and walked out. Ruth was absent from her desk.

As Emma walked down the hallway, she heard Thornton's booming voice, "Ruth, get in here!! Right now!"

The next night, Emma arrived early at Mug's Pub with two of her girlfriends. She gave Robert and Frank the thumbs up and took the booth in the back. Thornton stumbled in a half hour later. Emma told her friends to skedaddle.

"Go mingle with the natives for a while," Emma said. "I'll give a signal to Robert when I need you to return."

The girls emptied out of the booth as Thornton stumbled to the table.

"Oh, well, ladies, please don't leave on my account," Thornton flirted, slurring his words. "Please, stay and join my new friend Emma and me. The more the merrier."

The girls eyed Emma as if they were asking if she was OK. She smiled and nodded. Emma knew she was OK. She had her two girlfriends and Frank and Robert keeping a close eye on her if things got crazy. That's why she had picked the place. She also had told Amelia to stay as far away as possible.

"You're drunk," Emma said.

"You're a whore, just like your mother. We're even," Thornton said.

She let the comment fly and out of the corner of her eye, saw that Robert was monitoring. He had incredible hearing so she knew he was hearing all of this, sitting just a short distance from her playing his piano, pretending to be oblivious to anything that was going on in the bar.

"Tell me everything, now," Emma demanded.

"Oh, come on, let's just have a little fun for now," Thornton said. "Let's get to know each other, my long lost daughter that I never knew. Tell me about yourself."

Emma knew the evening's planned mission was aborted. She wasn't going to get anything substantial out of Thornton. She motioned for Frank.

"This man seems to be drunk off his rocker," Emma said. "Can you make sure he gets driven to that old motel at the outskirts of town tonight? Do not let him be taken home."

Emma suddenly felt protective of Amelia.

With that, Emma got up, whispered to Robert that they would discuss plan B tomorrow, and left the premises with her girlfriends.

There was no plan B. Yet. But the four conspirators decided to just keep Emma as a thorn in Thornton's side.

Emma, with her female friends in tow, appeared nearly everywhere Thornton appeared during his social time. If he was at Mug's Pub, they conspicuously arrived an hour later. Thornton undoubtedly would have knocked a few back by the time they arrived and he wanted to play with his female companions. So the friends played with James Thornton, stroking his ego and flirting shamelessly with the older man. They laughed and cajoled him. He soaked up the attention, even seemingly enjoyed his daughter's company.

Emma detested the act but was doing it for her new friend Amelia and for herself, and even for her own mother. It was time someone got the better of this conniver.

After about six months of the foolishness, Emma had had enough of the act. She upped the stakes in a private father-daughter dinner in which she made sure he drank just enough to be of sound mind and coherent, but also enough to loosen his lips. She told him that the fun was over if he didn't start bringing her in on his little schemes. Thornton pouted but he was having too much fun with the girls and had let his guard down.

"OK," Thornton said, after his fourth or fifth cocktail and a glaze had set in his eyes. "I'm amassing insanely massive amounts of money from various sources. You don't need to know the details. Then I'm fleeing this town and all the idiots who inhabit it. I'll give you a 10 percent cut."

"You'll give me 50 percent," Emma said without flinching.

"That's outrageous!" Thornton said. "I've done all the work and have been planning this for a long time. I created my own revenue sources and my own future. You're coming in on the tail end. You don't deserve that much. I'm only letting you in on this because you discovered what I was up to, and I can't exactly kill you."

"You will give me 50 percent to keep my mouth shut," Emma said. "I know where you are stealing all of your money from, what you call your sources of revenue. If you do not agree to those terms, I will tell anyone who will listen what you have been up to, including my mother and your precious Amelia. Everyone will know that I am the daughter you abandoned at birth. You will give me my cut of the money and you won't ever have to see or hear from me again."

Thornton stared at her for a long time with those mean, evil, cold-stone eyes. The vein in his forehead was bulging. Then he surprised Emma when he started to chuckle. The laughter increased until he had to pull off his spectacles and wipe away the tears from his eyes.

"You are good," Thornton said. "You are a chip off the old block, I guess. Well, I think we might be able to arrange some sort of partnership."

"How much money are we talking?" Emma asked.

"You're on a need-to-know basis right now, and right now, you don't need to know," Thornton said.

"I do need to know or deal's off," Emma said. "The town reads about everything in *The Main Informer*."

Thornton sighed. "OK, it's up to two million dollars and I plan to double that by next spring."

Emma gasped. She knew he was up to something but had never fathomed that they were talking about so much money.

"Where is it?" Emma asked.

"Oh, no, my dearest little....daughter," Thornton said. "That definitely is going to be kept secret until we are ready to pull up stakes and leave town."

"Who said I was leaving town?" Emma asked.

"If I give you a cut of the money, you most definitely will leave town and never utter a word of this to anyone here again," Thornton said. "That's my condition."

In her mind, Emma knew that he couldn't force her to do that. But she agreed to his "condition," at least to his face. She was envisioning him sitting in a jail cell.

"How do I know you won't just skip town now and leave me high and dry?" Emma said.

"You don't but I guess you'll just have to trust me, dear daughter," Thornton said.

Emma flinched at the "dear daughter" comment.

"One more thing," Emma said. "You will start paying for me to have a room at the luxurious Brass Inn hotel on Main Street."

Thornton resigned himself to giving in to this demand.

"Agreed," Thornton said. "But you do not utter a word of this to anyone and especially that you are my daughter. If you do, the deal is off."

The two shook hands to seal the agreement. Emma then wiped her hand on her skirt in disgust.

Emma later shared what she had learned with Amelia, Frank and Robert.

"We need to stop him before he extorts more money from me and the town's coffers," Amelia said. "Can't we do something right now?"

"What do you suggest?" Robert asked. "We can't go to the authorities. He's paying all of them off and the keepers of the town's coffers are in cahoots with him on some level. Let's just keep our eyes on him and let him lead us to the money. Sooner or later he's going to slip up and lead at least one of us to wherever he might be stashing it. I'm guessing he eventually will share his hiding place with Emma. This guy also is greedy. He's not going to scram until he has all of his money."

"How do we know if he's lying about how much money he has amassed?" Frank asked. "He might have more than that but just told Emma a lower figure. He might have doubled or tripled that already."

"In that case, he's going to steal even more from all of us," Amelia fretted.

"That's a possibility," Robert said. "In fact, it's a probability. If his original goal was to gather four million for himself and thinks he has to give Emma a million to go away, he's now going to need another two million dollars to cover the costs."

"This is sickening," Amelia said. "We can't let him continue doing this."

"Just relax," Robert said. "We will get all of the money back. Trust me. He's too greedy. We will monitor his actions and he eventually will screw up. He will lead us to the stash of cash."

"I still think we should try to find someone trusted with the authorities at least so they can help us," Amelia said. "After all, aren't we committing a crime ourselves by setting him up with this extortion plan?"

They all knew Amelia was right but for the moment, couldn't think of an alternative. Robert convinced them to just be patient and relax for the time being. They agreed to ponder over the next few days and weeks an appropriate approach and who they could trust and enlist to help.

By the time Harrison arrived in town on April 12, 1912, the foursome's plan was in full swing. In fact, Robert had hopes that it was nearing completion.

That's why Harrison had bumped into Emma at the hotel. The scene on the riverboat was all part of Emma's little charade as well. She had appeared to be one of Thornton's little girlfriends but really was his daughter, playing an elaborate scheme that four friends had hatched in desperation.

CHAPTER 28

After Thornton disappeared, Amelia still felt sorry for Emma, though Emma didn't want sympathy. She made it clear that she knew how to fend for herself and was a survivor. Still, Amelia tried in vain to get Emma to come to the school and benefit from some education.

"Let it be my gift to you and help provide you with some wonderful opportunities in your life," Amelia had pleaded.

Emma protested that it was too late, that she was too old and not teachable.

"Besides, I have all the street smarts that I need to get by in life," Emma had told Amelia.

Amelia had countered with "Yes, you are very smart street-wise and you are a survivor. But think of how much more you can accomplish with your life if you have the basic foundation of a good education. Think how far you can go when you combine your street smarts and toughness with the knowledge to back it up."

For the longest time, Emma could not be convinced. If she admitted it to Amelia and herself, it was because she was scared. She was scared of the unknown and scared of failing to live up to her own expectations but even more so to Amelia's expectations. She had seen firsthand how well Amelia related to her students and how smart all of them were, and how they were such proper young ladies, trained in etiquette and manners. Emma had never been taught any of that and she feared that the girls, who were much younger, would make fun of her.

As time went on, however, and Thornton seemingly was not returning, Emma finally came around.

Harrison's daughter, Penelope, also arrived at the school and strongly influenced Emma's awakening and desire to do more with her life. Emma had an instant and unexplainable connection to Penelope after Harrison was killed, taking an instant liking to the little girl. They connected on their own, unique level.

At first, Emma put on the tough girl front. She had never been given the opportunity to get a formal education. For the first 20 years of her life, she basically was just a survivor, scraping away and trying to pull herself out of poverty and a bad upbringing.

So Amelia started teaching her how to read, write, do arithmetic; she taught her manners and etiquette alongside all the other girls. She did this in the classroom setting but also spent extra time with Emma and her new little companion, Penelope.

Amelia also felt a special connection to both Penelope and Emma. In some ways, Amelia felt responsible for them. Her own plight had been responsible for bringing Emma to her and she had let Emma talk her into devising their scheme against her own father; Penelope's father had died as a result of Amelia's need for assistance in dealing with Thornton also.

"I am so sorry for what you had to go through, in your childhood and for what we made you do in trying to get back at your father," Amelia had told Emma at one point. "But I also am grateful that you entered my life at the point that you did. Your loyalty and friendship mean more to me than you can ever know."

"It's not your fault and I volunteered for the mission against my father," Emma said. "I absolve you of all responsibility for me and my life and my actions to this point. Now don't screw up the rest of my life."

Emma laughed nervously and Amelia laughed with her.

"And thank you for coming into my life, too," Emma acknowledged quietly, in a voice so soft and small that Amelia barely caught it. She embraced the younger woman in acknowledgement.

Amelia felt guilty that her actions ultimately led to both young girls losing their parents and needing a new structure in their lives. Emma was older and a survivor. Her plight had started long before she knew Amelia and Amelia knew that she would be OK.

But Amelia felt particularly guilty about Penelope's father dying because he was trying to help Damsel in Distress Amelia instead of staying at home to raise his daughter.

That situation was a bit more complicated to deal with than the relationship between Amelia and Emma. Amelia knew she would have to tread lightly and that one day she would have to have the dreaded conversation with Penelope in which she took responsibility for Harrison Parker's death. But for now, she focused on educating, training and developing the two girls into proper, educated young ladies.

While Emma was a little rough around the edges, Penelope had nary a sharp or jagged edge in her heart or soul. Amelia observed the unlikely pairing. It turned out to be a perfect match, in Amelia's opinion. While Emma taught Penelope how to be a strong woman, to stand up for herself, to be tough in the face of adversity, Penelope wormed her way into the depths of Emma's heart. Penelope taught Emma how to be a "little girl" at heart and to foster good and kindness not only in her own heart but in others.

"I'm having the childhood that I never had," Emma exclaimed one day when Amelia caught the duo playing hide-and-seek around the campus.

It struck Amelia how similar the two young girls were, despite a 14-year age gap and differing backgrounds. Both had essentially lost their parents – Emma's in abstention despite being alive, while both of Penelope's parents had been cruelly and suddenly ripped from her life all before she reached her 7th birthday. Despite differing circumstances, the two girls had a common bond—abandoned in their formative years, left to fend for themselves in ways that others they encountered had not experienced.

Amelia often saw Penelope and Emma hanging out together at the school, sharing lessons or some youthful girlie secret and even sillier girl giggles that resonated within the confines of the majestic trees hovering over the campus.

Others took note of the odd duo as well. Despite their physical age difference, they were learning the basics of math and reading and writing at the same level. Over time, they also learned how to grow up from their girlish mentality into young women.

Emma accelerated at her studies a little faster than Penelope and eventually was invited to become a teacher and mentor herself. Of course, the first student she personally mentored one-on-one was Penelope.

CHAPTER 29

Emma had some legitimate concerns about Amelia but she wasn't certain how to approach the topic. One day, when Amelia was alone at the gazebo, Emma approached her.

"Amelia, I have a question for you and forgive me for being so blunt," Emma said. "I, uh, well..."

Amelia turned around and looked at her curiously, with a caring smile.

"What is troubling you, my child?" Amelia asked.

"Well, I have been wondering what's wrong with you, to be honest," Emma said. "An out-of-town police detective that you seemed to become somewhat fond of in a relatively short amount of time, who happens to be the husband of one of your best friends, is killed. Yes, they said it was a suicide but you yourself don't believe that. And my own father, your husband, has vanished, seemingly without a trace. He has placed much trouble in your life and he could return to create even more havoc."

Amelia did not say anything and instead continued to smile at Emma, waiting patiently for her to finish.

"But you are completely unfazed by all of this," Emma said. "I don't understand how you can be going on about your life, moving on, as if nothing has happened and nothing can touch you or hurt you. It's like all of that is not troubling you as much as it is troubling me. We have a murderer in our midst and you appear to be nonplused."

Amelia stared at young Emma for a while, finally sighed and said, "My dear, sweet Emma. I am not completely unfazed by all that has happened in this little town and in particular to me and to you, for that matter. But you need to understand, I can't let it paralyze me, and truly, we don't have anything to worry about from here on out."

Emma gave her a bewildered look.

"Yes, I admit, I am extremely upset about Harrison's death and that it was the result of my plight," Amelia said. "If I had never sent those letters to dear Madeline and she hadn't died and her husband hadn't discovered them, none of this would have ever happened. He would still be alive to take care of that beautiful daughter of his. But I can't change what happened. I can only affect the present and the future. And I have a tremendous responsibility to all of these young girls at this school, as well as to you and to his daughter to continue my mission of teaching all of you to be strong, independent young women."

"But why aren't you worried about the murderer coming after us and the possibility of my father returning from wherever he went?" Emma asked. "That's what I'm most fearful of happening. I don't want him back in my life now that I see how good life can be. To be honest, I never thought this feeling was possible. And I was admittedly quite skeptical. But you were persistent and I do see the good in the world. But I can't help but wonder when all the evil and bad things will return. It's not possible to always be so happy and carefree and forget that people like my father are out there lurking and waiting to bring us down."

Amelia pondered Emma's words for quite some time. Then, choosing her words carefully, she spoke.

"My dear, I do not want you to spend your life worrying about such matters," Amelia said. "I can't tell you how I know this because I'm not really sure I know this, but I don't believe that James Thornton will bother either one of us ever again. Call it woman's intuition. But rest assured, that man will not be back in our lifetimes, and we both are better off for it."

"We also can't live our lives continually looking over our shoulders, wondering about what happened to Harrison," Amelia continued. "His murder has affected me a great deal. And yes, I believe it was murder and not suicide. But I try to not dwell on it because really, I can't change what happened."

CHAPTER 30

Amelia had worked hard to create and maintain her reputation as a prim and proper lady and because of that, some people, including her husband, had taken her for granted. Despite her delicate, feminine appearance and manners, she happened to be quite knowledgeable about worldly things. She had a quiet resolve and remained true to her principles no matter the task or challenge.

She ran a strict school, with the young ladies often referring to her as a gentle and soft-spoken mentor. She was firm but fair with the young ladies and could be strict with the rules when the situation required it.

"I am instilling in all of you what my mother instilled in me and what her mother instilled in her," Amelia told each new flock of students.

Of course, Amelia emphasized the education found in the textbooks and learned from teachers. But she broadened and enhanced that learning tool with real-life skills.

She taught, for example, things they would learn in finishing school.

Also adept at all things fashionable for the times, Amelia displayed expertise in what a proper lady should wear. She employed a strict set of standards of what was appropriate attire.

"Appearance and first impressions mean everything for a young lady's reputation," Amelia often told her students. "There shall be no display of your legs or cleavage. It only serves to invite trouble when a young lady shows off parts of her body that are sacred."

Emma, for one, laughed at this concept after having been raised basically in a place where clothing is optional. Still, Emma adhered to the rules out of respect for Amelia.

Amelia also enforced strict dating rules for the older girls, and dating was only allowed for the young ladies who reached the age of 16, the same age that Amelia was allowed to partake in such activities. Prior to attainment of that milestone age, however, beginning at a very early age, Amelia instilled in the children what it means to be a lady, and particularly in the presence of young men. She gave lessons on how to behave so as not to damage the reputation of the school but more importantly, not to damage their own reputations.

"Once you receive an undesirable label that should never be bestowed upon a respectable young lady, you will carry that label with you forever," Amelia reminded the girls. "Society is unforgiving in that matter."

In addition, any young man who made a social call to a young lady at the school was required to at least meet Amelia, although she preferred to include the parents in the visit when they were available. She fully believed in everyone being properly introduced and instilling in the young man that the lady he hoped to squire had a strong network of family support and love surrounding her if he felt inclined to get out of line.

As part of their lessons, the girls were taught the proper way to sit, stand and walk as a lady. They were taught the art of conversation, the proper way to set a table, host a luncheon or tea, host a dinner or charity balls. They also learned how to dance and conduct themselves in all kinds of social settings.

They ate on fine china and used silver table settings alongside crystal glasses.

"What is the point of keeping the good stuff tucked away and only brought out for special occasions?" Amelia asked the girls. "We not only need to learn proper etiquette but we also need to practice it each day."

Then one day Amelia decided to add another element to the student's education.

"What do you think about getting the girls together and forming a Girl Scout troop?" Amelia asked Emma.

"A what?" Emma said.

"Take a look at this newspaper article," Amelia said. "It says here that a Juliette "Daisy" Gordon Low gathered a group of girls together in Savannah, Ga., in March of 1912 and formed the 'Girl Scouts of the USA.' "

"So what does that mean?" Emma said. "The girls dress up in military uniforms and go out on scouting missions to look for, what, soldiers?"

"No, no, no..." Amelia said. "They do activities together and leaders teach the girls about the real world. It says here that the goal is to provide opportunities for the girls to develop physically, mentally and spiritually. They do it through community service and outdoor activities, such as camping."

"Sounds swell," Emma said. "Don't we already do charitable things?"

"Well, yes, but this is more structured and goal-oriented," Amelia said. "The girls receive first-hand knowledge of what they are learning. And there are handbooks for the leaders and the girls to work together."

Emma rolled her eyes.

"Come on, Emma, it could be fun and something different to do here," Amelia said. "I think our school is a perfect setting to establish a Girl Scout troop. It will enrich the educational experience so what can be wrong about that? It says here that we can plan camping trips, hiking excursions and play organized sports. They can also study first aid, homemaking, cooking, sewing and child-rearing. You and I might even learn something."

"I don't see the point," Emma said.

"You will," Amelia said. "The handbooks and uniforms should arrive any day now."

"Uniforms?" Emma said. "I'm not participating in any silly games or holding hands and singing goofy songs around a campfire, and I'm most certainly not wearing a uniform."

"You are going to have fun with this, young lady, trust me," Amelia said.

Emma just shook her head in resignation, because once Amelia had an idea in her mind, there was no further discussion.

And so it was that Amelia and Emma dressed up in their Girl Scout leader outfits and took the girls on excursions. They visited hospitals and nursing homes and even took field trips to government buildings to witness how their elected officials ran the local government as well as the state government. They also learned to ride horseback, side saddle as any proper lady would, of course - and ice skate and study birds. After all, there were many birds that inhabited the school's towering trees.

In addition to the Girl Scout activities, Amelia sometimes took small groups of the young ladies down to Main Street. They would don their large-brimmed bonnets trimmed with ribbons and flowers, and twirled their parasols in their white-gloved fingers as they took long, leisurely strolls. Amelia loved all of the action on Main Street and the girls loved the opportunity to purchase something special with their allowances. Main Street had an odd mingling of brand new vehicles with the old-fashioned carriages that were drawn by the most beautiful and gentle horses Amelia had ever seen. One could always observe true gentlemen squiring their ladies on their arms, enjoying each other's company. Amelia had lacked that type of companionship from her own husband but had not given up hope of finding it.

There was the enchanting smell of the coffee shop, where Amelia sometimes enjoyed the scent more than the actual taste. There also was the outdoor winery, but that trip was reserved for special days with Emma and some of the teachers. Sometimes the girls she had mentored at the school would come back as grown women, wives and mothers now. They would reminisce under the trees that hung over the outdoor brick-paved winery.

Finally, Amelia wanted to instill a sense of simplicity and the ability to find beauty in the smallest miracles of life.

Amelia sometimes woke the girls early so they could see the sunrise. They would hem and haw but in the end, they were in awe. She also took them to the highest land point of the school so they could watch the beautiful fiery orange sunsets.

"This is my favorite activity of all of the ones you drag me to," Emma told Amelia one evening. "The beauty of it all makes me shed a tear each time I witness a new sunset."

"Now Emma, are you being sarcastic again," Amelia said.

"Not this time," Emma said. "It is the most amazing thing I've ever seen, how it's different every night. I am in awe of nature's creation."

Amelia beamed inside and out at finally finding something that touched Emma's heart and soul.

CHAPTER 31

One day, Amelia got an idea to help Penelope remember her parents in a loving, positive way. She decided it would be nice for them to plant a gardenia bush, Madeline's favorite flower, on the school property. She allowed Penelope to pick the location.

"Is there such a thing as a sweet pea flower?" Penelope asked Amelia when she made the suggestion.

"Why yes there is, they are extremely colorful, beautiful flowers, too," Amelia said. "Do you want to add some of those to our garden as well?"

"Yes, please," Penelope said, delighted at the prospect. "My Daddy always called me his sweet pea. They would be wonderful to grow along with my Mommy's gardenias, wouldn't they?"

"Absolutely," Amelia agreed. "Why don't we head down to Main Street and visit my dear friend Catherine who owns the garden shop. She can help us pick out the gardenia and sweet pea plants and show us how to plant them and take care of them."

Within days, Catherine was at the school helping Amelia and Penelope plant the garden.

"The gardenia shrub needs to stay in partial shade and cooler temperatures," Catherine instructed them. "Despite the heat and humidity in this region, if you keep it in partial shade, it will thrive. In fact, gardenias love humidity and we all know there is no shortage of that here."

They planted two bushes, with a little bit of manual labor assistance from Frank and Robert, one on each side of the brick steps leading up to the main building of the school, the majestic one with four columns that everyone first witnesses as they are brought up the tree-lined drive.

"I love the scent that these pure white flowers emit," Penelope said. "No wonder my Mama loved them."

"Now the sweet pea flowers require full sun so why don't we plant the seeds for these along the outside of the gazebo," Catherine said. "They are vine-like flowers so they can grow up around the gazebo."

It was a perfect place as the gazebo was free from the shadows of the tall trees that adorned the rest of the campus. It sat almost on display in a valley of the campus where it received full sunlight most of the day.

Penelope enlisted Emma's help to tend to her gardens, making sure they received the proper watering, trimming and fertilizing.

Penelope adored the wide variety of colors that the sweet peas displayed – pink, blue, white, purple and red. She loved to cut them after they had matured to their full potential and adorn the tables in the dining hall with her arrangements. She also loved to surprise Amelia and Emma sometimes with a bouquet on their desks of the sweet peas with a gardenia placed in the middle.

"They make your offices smell so pretty," Penelope said.

But then the flowers suddenly started vanishing from Amelia's desk. Not wanting to alarm Emma or Penelope, or any of the girls, Amelia mentioned it to Frank and Robert instead.

"You both are going to think I'm crazy, but Penelope occasionally brings flowers to Emma and me from her gardenia and sweet pea garden," Amelia said. "But now all of a sudden, the flowers from my vase keep disappearing."

"Are Emma's gone, too, or just yours?" Robert asked.

"Just mine," Amelia said. "I check her desk when my go missing. But don't tell her, or Penelope, because I don't want to alarm them, or anyone else."

"Perhaps it's just the housecleaning ladies removing them, thinking they're dead," Frank said.

Amelia shook her head no.

"I can't afford housekeepers right now so I'm doing the cleaning," Amelia said.

"Have you noticed anything else weird going on," Robert said.

"Well, when I get up in the morning and am waiting for my tea water to heat up, I like to gaze out on the property from my kitchen window," Amelia said. "I sometimes think I see someone or something lurking from tree to tree but then they just vanish. And I convince myself it's just my imagination, or a large animal."

"I thought that was just one time," Robert said.

"It has happened again a few times lately," Amelia said. "But I was trying not to worry about it and didn't want to bother you with it because the last time, it turned out to be nothing. It's probably just a large animal."

"This is an order, you let me or Robert know the next time you see something. Immediately," Frank said.

CHAPTER 32

"Arson!" declared the Tirtmansic Fire Department's fire marshal about the fire that nearly destroyed Mug's Pub in 1925. Frank had just left the pub around midnight. He lived a couple blocks over on Third Street but when he heard the sirens and saw flames in the brisk, dark sky, he knew that it was someone's building on Main Street and he had to go help. So he rushed back to find the second floor of his beloved building fully engulfed.

The fire destroyed the second floor but miraculously, the bar area sustained just smoke and water damage. With some coaxing from Amelia and Robert, he decided the best thing to do was to rebuild.

However, the fire did not even reach the alcohol that Frank was serving his patrons–illegally. Frank had figured out that prohibition was coming so in the late 1910s, he did what he could to stock up on alcohol. The product was stashed in the tunnels that ran underneath the pub and to some establishments along Main Street. Only a handful of people knew of their existence, including Robert.

For 14 years, while America lived under the law of prohibition, Frank kept the local law enforcement at bay. This was partly due to

Robert's unknown connections in the police department and partly due to Det. Cutter returning to Tirtmansic as a private investigator. Cutter constantly reminded the Tirtmansic Police Department how they had messed up the investigation of his partner's death so they left Frank and his establishment alone.

Frank also had made sure that Mug's Pub became the favored hangout for the local firefighters and police officers. Therefore, trouble, for the most part, remained at bay. However, around 1924, Frank had started sensing another kind of trouble, with strangers wandering in and asking questions of the locals. These seedy characters were making Frank uneasy.

To the average observer or tourist in town, Mug's Pub had remained a rustic place to grab a decent homemade meal. It remained a dark, drab establishment except the alcohol did not flow as steadily as it had pre-prohibition. Frank had established a private, exclusive area on the second floor, where invited guests—men and women—could gather secretly to imbibe and revel in the camaraderie that the pub had provided for so many years. Only certain patrons even knew the private area existed, as the doorway leading back to the area was labeled "pantry." And a separate side entrance through the alleyway provided cover for those who were willing to test the reach of the law.

There were a few token raids of Mug's Pub from the feds but the raids usually came up empty. For reasons Frank and Amelia could never figure out, Robert always seemed to sense when a raid was impending and they usually had enough time to hide the alcohol beneath the building.

With all the protections and safeguards in place, Frank, Robert, Cutter and Amelia still wondered how the feds even knew they were serving alcohol to their patrons. Certainly they had been careful about who they allowed into the inner circle. Not all patrons were given the VIP treatment. But the patrons who did know about it were treated to the Roaring '20s style of entertainment, complete with a saloon-type atmosphere.

The little mystery of how the feds were finding out about Mug's Pub violating the law was enough to pull Cutter out of his funk for a while. After a few raids, Cutter and Robert teamed up to find out where their leak was located.

Then the fire happened. The firefighters were able to control most of the damage in the front dining area–along with all of the oddball trinkets and knickknacks. And with a lot of hard work and determination, along with the help of Amelia, Robert, Emma and Cutter, Frank was able to reopen Mug's Pub in a few months' time.

The fire marshal found burned papers and discarded gardenias and sweet peas in a trash can where he deduced that the fire had started. Yet higher-ups at the Tirtmansic Police Department did not pursue an investigation, calling it an accident. The police never told Cutter or Robert about the flowers.

"So Frank, does your wife like gardenias and sweet peas? It's my wife's birthday and I was thinking of giving her some of those flowers I found in the trash can upstairs after the fire," the fire marshal said one day while eating lunch at the bar.

"What flowers?" Frank and Robert asked simultaneously.

CHAPTER 33

Penelope's maternal grandparents became her legal guardians upon Harrison's death and they often made the trip to visit Penelope at the school. She took holiday at her grandparents' home and they often invited Amelia and Emma to join them.

When they also passed on, they appointed Lance Cutter to arrange for Amelia to take guardianship of Penelope.

So it was no surprise that the school was abuzz when a blessed event arrived. Robert Woodson's son, Robert Woodson The Second, had asked Amelia's and Cutter's permission to take Penelope's hand in marriage. By now, Penelope was a teacher and mentor at the school.

"Of course the answer is yes," both had said.

"But you better ask Penelope, too, just to make sure she will have you," Cutter had teased the young man.

Amelia and Emma were ecstatic to be asked to serve as surrogate co-mothers to help Penelope plan all the details.

The wedding was held in the chapel that had been built on the school grounds after Penelope's arrival. It had an extraordinary organ, which Robert Woodson I played throughout the ceremony.

"Would you do me the honor of walking me down the aisle?" Penelope asked Cutter. "You are the closest thing to my father and it would warm my heart to have you by my side as I enter my new life."

"I would be honored and privileged to walk you down the aisle," Cutter told her. "I could never fill your father's shoes but I will do my best to make you proud."

Cutter beamed almost as much as the bride as he held out his arm for the beautiful new bride. Aside from quitting alcohol, at least for the duration of the wedding festivities, Cutter had surprised Penelope with one of the greatest gifts of all.

"I hear from the ladies that there is a tradition of something old and something borrowed that a bride must have on her wedding day," Cutter told her. "My wife and I kept your mother's wedding dress over the years, thinking that one day you might want to have it to wear on your own wedding day."

Penelope shrieked with joy when Cutter and his wife produced it for her. The wedding also was a gift for the others, as it was one of the few times that Amelia, Emma and Penelope had seen Cutter so happy since his partner had died so many years prior.

In addition to wearing her mother's wedding dress, Penelope held her parents close to her heart with a bouquet of gardenias and colorful sweet peas. Penelope's students served as her bridesmaids and flower girls.

For the reception, Frank shut down Mug's Pub to celebrate the occasion. He and his wife, Lila, even went as far as giving it a good scrubbing to make it, well, as presentable as possible given it was a dark, dank, musty bar where patrons regularly spilled their drinks on the floor and smoked until a haze blanketed the place. Lila, Amelia and Emma had so much fun decorating the place and transformed it into such a beautiful venue that Frank seriously considered keeping it that way.

***

A few weeks before the wedding, Penelope asked Amelia about her parents. When she was younger, Penelope had begged Amelia and

Emma as well as her grandparents over and over again to tell her the beautiful love story about her parents. Amelia had shared with her what Madeline had written about in her letters, bragging about her beautiful family. But Amelia did not know where those letters were now so she could show them to Penelope; the letters had disappeared when Harrison died.

"I know you told me basically what happened," Penelope said. "But I think you have been trying to protect me and are withholding information about what really happened, especially to my father. I have heard so many wonderful things from everyone about my father, what a great man he was, how conscientious he was and how he had a strong sense of values and principles and family. So I cannot seem to reconcile in my mind how it was possible that he accidentally shot himself."

"I know, I know, my dear," Amelia said. "I have never been able to fully wrap my mind around the circumstances surrounding your father's death. I only know what I found out about him from your mother's letters and his brief stay here in Tirtmansic. I can assure you that everything you have heard, all of your life, from everyone who loves you, is that your father was exactly the man of whom everyone speaks. I have never believed it was an accident but unfortunately, the local authorities did not have much interest in pursuing the truth. Your dear Uncle Lance tried to find justice for your father. It just wasn't meant to be."

Penelope was not satisfied with that but she didn't know what else to do.

"The best thing that you can do for your parents now is to not dwell on how they died, but instead, focus on how they lived their lives," Amelia said. "They loved each other so much and it is so rare to find that kind of love. They also loved and cherished you with every ounce of their hearts. Now carry on that family tradition, honor their memories by loving and cherishing and honoring your husband-to-be with as much life and laughter as your heart can contain."

And Penelope did exactly that. Robert the Second and Penelope went on to live a long and loving life, bearing two sons and a daughter. Penelope now would be 86 years old but died when she was 76, some say of heartbreak after her beloved Robert died.

***

At the wedding reception, one of the guests sauntered over to Cutter, offered him a fine brandy and whispered appreciation for how he had handled the whole Thornton-Harrison matter. Although Cutter had sworn off alcohol for the evening, he couldn't turn down the drink. The guest was grateful that Cutter had gone along with the official report that Harrison had died accidentally. The guest also detailed things about the fire that had nearly destroyed Mug's Pub all those years ago.

Cutter pretended to play along, laughing and chatting so that none of the other guests would suspect anything awkward about the discussion. He didn't want to ruin Penelope's beautiful wedding day.

Shortly after the exchange, Cutter excused himself and headed back to the hotel. He collapsed on the cobblestone street in front of The Brass Inn. His death was ruled a heart attack, and in keeping with the tradition of the quirky little town of Tirtmansic, the case was officially closed.

CHAPTER 34

Inspired by what she had read about Margaret Brown, or as the world knew her, "The Unsinkable Molly Brown," Amelia got herself appointed to the school's Board of Trustees after Thornton disappeared. Margaret Brown, whom her friends and colleague called Maggie, may have been most well-known for her heroics during the *Titanic* disaster, but she also was one of the first women in the United States to run for political office, running for Senate eight years before women in America had the right to vote.

Some of the curmudgeonly old men begrudgingly voted in favor of allowing Amelia on the town's board because they were loyal to Thornton and didn't like the ruckus Amelia created about property taxes. However, with some perseverance and determination, Amelia prevailed, with a little help from her allies on the board.

They convinced the others that if Thornton reappeared and could finish the term, then it would be an easy transition to put him back in the seat. So Amelia was sworn in with all the pomp and circumstance that befalls a new public official and was appointed to sit on the board for the next three years, until 1915.

However, there was one hitch to her being a public servant. Women did not have the right to vote or be elected to office until the 19th Amendment to the U.S. Constitution was ratified in 1920, allowing women to vote and hold elected office. The women's suffrage movement was in full swing in the country and while she technically could have been jailed for even casting a vote on the board, it was allowed after much discussion and consternation.

Amelia could not run for re-election, but after serving her three years as a town trustee, she decided it was time to move on anyway. She knew she had accomplished at least one of her goals and despite their reluctance, the others on the Tirtmansic Board of Trustees had gained a tremendous amount of respect for this vibrant woman.

Specifically, Amelia had devised some creative ideas on how to cut the budget without slashing public services and had carefully studied and examined every aspect of every issue–whether it was a planning and zoning matter or an increase in salary for the sanitation workers – before she cast a vote. And when she argued her points to get the others to vote in her favor, they listened and sometimes she even persuaded them to side with her.

Dealing with Amelia Thornton had been much different than dealing with James Thornton, who never pondered the issues for the greater good of the community, but only for the greater good of James Thornton.

During her term and after she finished her service, Amelia used her experience as a learning tool. She introduced her students to the inner workings and functions of city government, public service and duties and responsibilities of being a trusted and respected elected official.

"It's only a matter of time when women will be able to cast their own votes and be elected to all levels of government," Amelia told her students.

***

When Amelia began her three years of public service, one of the first projects she embarked on was the town's property tax assessment system. She was inspired by Robert Woodson to examine the issue, from the assessments to the collection method for the funds and subsequent appropriation of those funds. Robert had been helping Frank on the business side and saw firsthand the burden of taxes on the business.

Robert and Amelia teamed up to discuss the issue with other business owners and even residents.

"From what we have been able to deduce, it seems that we all are paying an exorbitant amount in property taxes and not getting the highest level of services in return for our money," Amelia told a gathering of townsfolk any chance she got.

Robert and Amelia knew something fishy was going on but did not alert the citizens until they had concrete proof.

They discovered that nearly everyone in Tirtmansic was being charged more than they should be for their property taxes. And they discovered it was because of Thornton and the town's elected assessor. They found out that Thornton was in cahoots with the assessor and both had been taking kickbacks from the overcharges.

Robert and Amelia discovered that their unlikely pairing made them well-suited to work together. They bounced ideas off each other and what one lacked in knowledge on an aspect of the research, the other one could understand and analyze.

It proved to be an overwhelming task but Amelia was more determined than ever, especially after she discovered her own husband perpetuated and was a large part of the problem.

She and Robert spent countless hours, weeks and months familiarizing themselves with the tax laws. They learned methods from other states and cities, and how complicated and convoluted the system was.

"That's probably by design, so the average citizen has no clue they are being cheated," Robert told Amelia. "Officials also probably know that the average citizen will lose patience and give up trying to weave their way through the system."

Robert and Amelia finally determined that the system was failing its citizens and needed to be reformed. There were not equitable assessments across the board and there were different formulas for agricultural land, homesteads and businesses.

While in office, Amelia oversaw a complete revamping of the program. The assessor had been working at the will of the board; but the duo concluded that perhaps it was time for him to work at the will of the people.

The people also didn't know they had the right to appeal their assessments. The information was available for the citizens on how to go about doing it, but the town officials certainly never attempted to make it known. So Amelia enlisted the help of a reporter at *The Main Informer* to alert the citizens of their rights and to explain in laymen's terms the assessment system and how it was going to be reformed.

The results of the research were not met with much approval from some of Tirtmansic's governmental officials, particularly the town's assessor.

CHAPTER 35

Although Robert Woodson, the original piano man at Mug's Pub, had died long before Meghan Murphy was "formally" introduced to him in 1992, she did gain his acquaintance in a decidedly unlikely manner. One day after arriving at work, she noticed a green glow emanating from her office. She flipped the light switch in her office to the "on" position and walked around to the other side of the desk. Normally at the beginning of her work day, she would reach for the "on" button of her computer. But clearly someone else had taken care of that.

What appeared to be an essay was on the screen. The green text on the black computer monitors usually gave the reporters a headache if they looked at the screen too long. Her computer essentially was a glorified word processor. The only real difference between it and a typewriter was that if she made a mistake, White-Out wasn't required to fix it. The computer erased all evidence of the mistake with the stroke of the delete or back space keys. Everyone was amazed by the new technology.

Meghan had no idea who had written the story now appearing on her screen, but she sat down to read it nonetheless. It did not have a byline but something else struck her right away.

The dateline read: *Tirtmansic, April 15, 1912*. She checked her calendar, just to reassure herself that it was 1992.

Following the dateline was a lengthy introduction:

My name is Robert Woodson. I am a piano player at Mug's Pub on Main Street in Tirtmansic. At least that is what everyone in town thinks I am. Only one other person, besides my wife, knows my real job and my real mission. I am a private detective and I have been hired to keep an eye on a certain individual. I have been following this person for the better part of a year and I am close to solving this crisis that this individual has imposed on this town.

The sad thing is that this person has created immense financial problems for the entire town and most of the people don't even know it. Only a handful of bright individuals realize what this individual is up to and we have formed a somewhat unlikely alliance to work toward bringing this man to justice. Only one of the four knows my true identity, although I suspect that one sweet, fancy lady might have figured out there is more to me than meets the eye.

Have I piqued your interest? Do you want to know more about this mystery? I will walk you through most of it but I need your help to solve the final piece of the puzzle. My friend Harrison Parker, who unfortunately became a victim of this tragic situation, begs for assistance as well.

Please keep reading if you are interested in knowing more about this most intriguing of stories that hopefully will reach a conclusion in the very near future.

Meghan sat paralyzed in her seat. Who was Robert Woodson and why was this dated 80 years ago, on the exact same day as the sinking of the *Titanic*? Why was it on her computer and how had someone written it seemingly in present day on a modern computer?

Meghan was curious and inquisitive by nature so she indeed wanted to know more. She was afraid that the story unfolding on her computer screen might vanish so she hit the print button to preserve a hard copy. Then she returned to reading.

This Robert Woodson detailed how he and Frank Henderson, the owner of Mug's Pub, had been helping the bright, energetic and unflappable Amelia Adams Thornton with her plight for more than a year. It also detailed the story and background of the lovely Emma Thornton.

Even the keenest observer sees me just as a piano-playing fool, Robert wrote. *I admit I enjoy playing the piano, even when I'm not doing it for a paycheck. In fact, I enjoy the spontaneous sessions that some of the patrons request when I'm not technically on duty. I quietly go about my business but unbeknownst to most, while I am perched on my piano bench, I am in a fine position to observe all the people who come into Mug's Pub. I observe who comes and goes, when and how often. I have incredible hearing and I am able to pick up snippets of most conversations. Some are just downright rumors and gossip with no purpose and they make me chuckle to myself. But every once in a while I hear something of value.*

"I have a lot of great ideas and could solve more than half of the people's problems if they would just ask me for advice," Woodson wrote. "Admittedly, some are lame but some are downright genius. But half the time, nobody even acknowledges my presence save for my music, let alone listens or pays attention to me. But they should. Particularly about this individual who certainly is in line to ruin the town and their livelihoods.

That was all the tease Meghan received on her computer that day. And sure enough, as soon as she finished reading, the screen went blank.

Meghan re-read the message she had saved in hard copy form several times over the next few days and hoped each day upon her arrival at work that a new message might appear. After a week, she gave up hope of receiving anymore news.

CHAPTER 36

Meghan came up behind him as he sat at his desk and gently caressed the back of his neck with her long fingers that were made for piano playing. She ran her hands through his newly-buzzed hair at the nape of his neck, working her way up to cup the back of his head. She reached down, allowing her breasts to lightly touch his back, then leaned in to blow in his ear and then softly nibble the top of his ear.

"Wow!" he thought to himself. "Such a small gesture but so incredibly hot and erotic."

He reached behind him to grab at her waist as she came around to sit in front of him on the edge of the desk. She stood with her legs slightly open, teasing him with what lay underneath, in the shadows beneath her skirt.

Then he grabbed her and sat her sideways on his lap and she continued to rub her hands through his hair as she reached up with her mouth, searching for his. She gently teased his closed lips with her tongue until they parted and their tongues met. She continued to tease him gently until the passion overtook both of them and their tongues lunged at each other, tasting, seeking each other, deeper into each other.

Her bosom was billowing out of her fire engine red bra, her nipple piercing through the fabric, searching, seeking his touch, aching for his fingers and his wet tongue. He reached underneath her blouse and massaged her back with his strong, manly hands. He caressed her spine, from the nape of her neck to the end of her spine, where his fingers touched the tops of her lace panties. His light touch sent giddy goose bumps up and down her body. Although he had not touched her there yet, the feeling reached down into the depths of her womanhood below.

While she was enjoying that thrill, he reached up and unhooked her bra with the finesse of a man who had done this before. He taunted her with caresses along her upper back and around to her side, just barely brushing the sides of her breasts. She started unbuttoning her blouse and opened it in time for him to reach his head down and suckle on her left nipple, before she could even remove the bra straps to fully free her upper body from the trappings of its garments.

Meghan woke up with a start. She thought she felt someone actually caress her back. But that could not be, could it? The last thing she remembered was reading Robert Woodson's note again. She convinced herself that she must have fallen asleep and simply was dreaming. But who was the guy? It took her a few minutes to gather her bearings.

Then she asked herself, "Was it a dream? Was it a ghost or was it real?"

Once she was more awake, she realized that it would be impossible to have such an experience with a ghost.

"Wouldn't it?" she asked herself.

But then again, she had been having ghost-like encounters lately. Was she just feeling lonely and craving the attention of a man? Had her sub-conscious transported her back to a simpler, old-fashioned, more chivalrous era because of her recent brushes with things that had happened 80 years ago? But certainly, men and women didn't carry on like that 80 years ago, did they?

Meghan felt her cheeks and they seemed feverish, although she knew she was not sick. She was burning up from the hotness of the dream, or whatever it was.

"Oh, just push it out of your mind, Meghan, and get a grip," said told herself. "First you're hearing ghosts and receiving messages from them, now you think they're making love to you. I really am sick in the head!"

Meghan rubbed the sleep out of her eyes and called her investigator friend Nick Gravinski. Nick always had a different view of things and never did things by the book. He never planned anything and never thought through to the end of something. He just knew that the ending would write itself, and he would deal with it when it arrived.

But she knew if she presented this entire scenario to him, far-fetched as it might seem - from the clicking sounds on the bricks to the note about Harrison Parker; the sounds of the piano inside a vacant Mug's Pub; her wine glass being knocked over seemingly by a spirit; the *Titanic* boarding pass flying inexplicably out of her hand; the message on her computer; to perhaps even the dream–that he would help her unravel the mystery behind all of it.

But first she would have to endure his skepticism and teasing. He didn't believe in ghosts or spirits driving a person to some foregone conclusion. She would have to overcome that to convince him to help her.

She also wasn't sure if she should mention any of this to her publisher and editor.

Meghan realized that her sources in this instance were, of all things, ghost-like. She never revealed her sources, even when her editor was persistent and even downright threatening in asking her to reveal them. But she knew if she ever told anyone their identities, her sources would dry up. She never told a soul. And in this case, if she told anyone her sources might just be ghosts, she would be locked away in the loony bin.

Basically, she needed solid evidence and proof of something

strange going on that supposedly had occurred 80 years ago. She needed corroboration of the facts, if nothing else, to give herself peace of mind and maybe end these odd encounters.

CHAPTER 37

Meghan sat at a table in one of the odd sunrooms at Mug's Pub. She tapped the ashes off her dainty cigar and lifted her wine glass to the bartender to indicate she needed a refill.

A myriad of papers were scattered all over the table. There were newspaper clippings about Annabelle Adams' School for Young Ladies, stories from other newspapers about the Mercy Angels Nursing Home, and the first story that she had written for *The Main Informer*.

She cringed as she re-read the article about Mrs. Spencer that somehow had accidentally made its way into the pile. She had tried to bury the story from her mind but she acknowledged that it was a reminder of what not to do when interviewing a subject. She had been a naïve, cub reporter at the time of that interview. She admitted only to herself that she had no idea what she was doing when she accepted her first reporting job.

She had been sent to the nursing home to interview a woman who was turning 100 years old, a major milestone, of course. Meghan at first balked at the idea of interviewing a 100-year-old woman. She had a pre-conceived notion that the woman would be incoherent, drooling and staring off into space the whole time. But Meghan had found something much different, an incredibly alert, dear woman whom everyone at the nursing home referred to affectionately as Mrs. Spencer. It was a feel-good fluff piece about one of the community's few centenarians. At the time, Meghan had designs on being a hard-hitting, investigative reporter. But early in her career, her editor sent her on these low-intensity assignments.

The intent was to write a heart-warming retrospective of the woman's life, the secret to longevity and so on. But Meghan realized only later that she had let her subject control the interview. It was her first lesson as a journalist, and one she never forgot.

Although the rest of the woman's body was aged and frail, the woman's youthful eyes had struck Meghan from the moment she met her. As the photograph from the decaying newspaper article stared back at Meghan, she still could see the woman's stunning blue eyes. Meghan also remembered that despite her age, the woman had a mind full of knowledge and the wisdom, energy and memory of a 20-year-old.

Each time Meghan tried to focus on something about her life, Mrs. Spencer had redirected her and focused on something that had happened in society or the world during that timeframe in her life. Her subject had talked in general about the world at large, but barely allowed Meghan to peek into her own life.

Meghan did not even realize how little she had garnered until she sat down to write the piece and noticed she knew absolutely nothing about the woman. Nonetheless, she wrote a glowing story about the last 100 years from the woman's perspective and her editor had loved it. He never even questioned the fact that it did not focus on the woman's life, but instead focused on life around the woman for the previous 100 years. He seemed to like her perspective and insight more than knowing about the woman behind the comments.

Meghan had kept telling herself, after she had learned a few things about interviewing and reporting, that she would go back and try to get the woman to talk about her own life.

Meghan decided that now might be the perfect time to pay that visit. She needed to check things out at the nursing home anyway, for her investigative piece.

Then the thought occurred to her that the woman might not still be alive. If she was, she would be 105 by now.

She could have called her newfound friend Rebecca to help her see the woman, but she didn't want to get her friend in trouble. Employees already were on guard at the nursing home because of that whole embarrassing IRS investigation that now seemed to have gone away. The next day, Meghan just showed up and inquired at the nurses' station of the Mercy Angels Nursing Home about Mrs. Spencer. She met some resistance until she showed the nurse the article she had written five years ago.

"This was the first article I ever wrote for the newspaper and she taught me a valuable lesson," Meghan told the nurse. "I came across it and wanted to see if she is still alive and willing to talk to me again. As I recall, she was an intriguing woman and seemed so full of life. She has been an inspiration to me all these years and I just want to say thank you if possible."

The nurse called the administrator to ask if it was OK to let Meghan Murphy from *The Main Informer* visit Mrs. Spencer. After a pause, the nurse hung up and led her to the woman's room, the same one where Meghan had sat with her five years prior. This time, the woman was bedridden, as was her roommate. But the old woman's eyes lit up when she saw Meghan; the roommate scowled, and Meghan didn't know why.

"I've been hoping you would come back to see me someday, young lady," Mrs. Spencer told Meghan. "I've been reading your articles in the newspaper. You have developed into quite the adept reporter over the years. I am proud of you."

Meghan was taken aback by this revelation.

"Don't look so surprised," the elderly woman said as she struggled to raise her bed and sit up a little straighter. The nurse helped her and said she would stay. But Mrs. Spencer waved her away and said "It's OK, my dear. This young lady is a friend."

Meghan sat silent for a moment, not sure what to say.

"Well, I, uh, have to say I am surprised," Meghan said. "That article I wrote was horrendous. I'm surprised you would even remember it. I only remember it because you taught me something valuable that day. I had let you control the interview and I learned to never do that again. And I learned that I found out nothing about you, the person, when I interviewed you."

Mrs. Spencer chuckled and said, "I know, dear. I did that on purpose. I knew you were green, as they say, and I wanted to teach you that you need to look below the surface if you are going to be a good reporter."

"Once a teacher, always a teacher," said the voice from the bed on the other side of the room.

The comment startled Meghan but she tried to ignore the other woman.

"I realized the moment I went to write the piece that I didn't have enough material to write about you, the person," Meghan said. "I didn't have time to come back and interview you, though. I had a strict deadline and the editor was breathing down my neck so I knew I had to write something. I made the most of it and surprisingly, my editor loved it for some reason. To this day, I'm not sure why."

"It was a good piece, despite the fact I didn't give you anything to work with," the kind woman said warmly. "I had hoped you would have returned sooner to see me, though. It took you long enough. This body could have given out and you wouldn't have had the opportunity to seek what you need."

Meghan was perplexed and not quite sure what Mrs. Spencer meant.

"Seek what I need?" Meghan said.

"Let me call for an orderly to come help me and my dear friend here into our wheelchairs and we'll go have a chat in the garden," Mrs. Spencer said.

The roommate glanced at Mrs. Spencer uneasily but the old woman just winked at her roommate.

Outside was a lush garden. Meghan was in awe of the colorful display of sweet peas and gardenias.

When the ladies were settled, Meghan asked, "That teacher comment inside. Did you happen to teach at Annabelle Adams' School for Young Ladies?"

The women exchanged a look and the still nameless roommate said in a not-so-friendly tone, "What do you know about that school?"

"Just what I have read in newspaper clippings, mostly favorable," Meghan said, wondering why the roommate was so unfriendly.

Mrs. Spencer shot her friend a look and she backed off.

"Let's start over," the old woman said. "I knew that Harrison eventually would try to make contact with you and bring you to me."

Meghan's jaw dropped. She usually had a poker face, revealing nothing. This tidbit shocked Meghan.

"Harrison?" Meghan said, trying to gain her composure.

"I believe he contacted me about six months ago," the woman said. "Am I correct that you know who I'm talking about, dear?"

"Um, Detective Harrison Parker?" Meghan asked hesitantly.

"Yes," Mrs. Spencer said.

"But he's dead," Meghan said. She almost added, "and would be really old by now," but noted her current audience.

"Yes, dear, he is, but his spirit remains," the old woman said. "I think he attempted to contact me throughout the years but I never realized it until the incident six months ago."

"What incident?" Meghan said.

"One day six months ago, the nursing home's manicurist came in to do our nails," Mrs. Spencer said. "The three of us–the manicurist, my roommate and I—were sitting at the table chatting about the weather or some nonsense. Then suddenly, we were startled by the noise of my bottle of nail polish. It was sitting on my nightstand, on the other side of the bedroom, and just fell over by itself. It was a round, full bottle, with a fat, rounded base and a smaller rounded top that was not easily knocked over, even with the force of a hand."

"We all sat there wide-eyed and stunned," the roommate said. "We all looked around the room to see if anyone else was there and there wasn't. None of us had seen anyone walk in and the door remained wide open, as it had been all day. The window was shut so there was no sudden gust of wind or air tunnel created."

"The manicurist tried jumping up and down near the nightstand to see if she could make it fall over," Mrs. Spencer said. "She pounded her fist on the nightstand. It was quite a sight, come to think of it. But the thing would not budge. It simply would not move without assistance. I think the docs wanted to commit us to the psych ward but all three of us had witnessed the same thing, thankfully. If I had just witnessed it myself, I know they would have locked me up."

"So? A bottle of nail polish falling over doesn't prove anything," Meghan said, skeptically, yet knowing deep down she was experiencing similar weird happenings. But she did not reveal this to her audience.

"Not in and of itself, you are right, dear," Mrs. Spencer said. "But I started receiving notes on my nightstand and we started hearing someone's voice in the middle of the night, and it wasn't in our own feeble minds. Our activities director, who is just as crazy as us, by the way, sat in with us one night and heard it, too. She is the reason we aren't in the loony bin – yet – because she is a believer as well. Most of the people around here just think we're a bunch of old biddies who are imagining things and they just laugh at us. They think it's all just silly. But we know better."

Meghan knew the activities director; her new acquaintance and friend Rebecca.

"You know for sure that it's this Harrison Parker, a detective?" Meghan said.

"Harrison and his partner, not his detective partner, but Robert Woodson, the piano player at Mug's Pub," Mrs. Spencer said. "You know him, too, of course, dear, right? Or you will soon enough, I suspect."

Meghan didn't acknowledge anything.

"I hoped that their spirits would reach out to you because if anyone could help reveal the truth, it would be you," Mrs. Spencer said.

"Why would you think that? And how do you know Harrison

Parker and Robert Woodson?" Meghan asked.

"I have been following your work and you are an excellent investigator," Mrs. Spencer said. "You can solve this 80-year-old mystery once and for all. I know you can. We need it solved and it appears that Harrison and Robert want you to be the one to end the mystery."

Meghan smiled and said, "Thanks for the vote of confidence but I'm not really a crime reporter. I leave the police work to the police. I do more of the paper trail type of investigating. And besides, you have first-hand knowledge of my inability to investigate even the simplest things, like interviewing you when you turned 100 years old. Anyway, back to what we were discussing. How do you know Harrison and Robert?"

The elderly woman paused, winked and then said, "Well, my dear, part of my namesake was the name of the school."

Meghan was genuinely perplexed–and curious–now.

"My real name is Amelia Annabelle Adams. Imagine learning to write and say that one when you're just a tyke," Amelia Annabelle Adams Thornton Spencer said. "After the scoundrel, James Thornton, disappeared or died, or whatever happened to him, and years later after I sold the school property to these nursing home folks, I met a wonderful man named Chris Spencer and we married. I became Amelia Spencer. Everyone here knows me as Amelia Spencer and most people don't make the connection that I am Amelia Adams, nor do most people care at this point. In fact, most people probably don't even know that this used to be my family's property and that I ran a school here on this very land. I'm 105 years old and although I am mentally as sharp as I was when I was 20, I know my body is failing me and fast. I need the truth before I die."

Again, Meghan was stunned into silence. She finally spoke.

"About James and whether he died, or just disappeared?" Meghan said.

"That, and more importantly, who killed Harrison? He was a beautiful young man with such promise. He had the most adorable young daughter," Amelia smiled in remembrance. "Such tragedy in his life and for his daughter. He needs to be put to rest. I want resolution for him more than anyone. I believe he is seeking that now from us and we need to do what we can to let him rest in peace."

"Uh, what exactly happened to Harrison?" Meghan asked hesitantly.

"Well, he was found dead in his hotel room, on the cusp of solving the mystery about James," Amelia said. "You are familiar with the room where he died, as a matter of fact."

"I am?" Meghan said.

"Your current office at *The Main Informer*," Amelia said. "The building used to be a very swanky hotel, called The Brass Inn. Look it up at the Historical Society. The room in which Harrison was found now is your own personal office. It's on the second floor at the end, right? You still can see the faded numbers in the paint on the door, can you not?"

"212," Meghan uttered in astonishment. She had tried to cover it up with paint but the numbers kept bleeding through. Now she knew why. And how did Amelia know which one was Meghan's personal office?

"The mystery has long been forgotten around here but you have an interest in it, don't you?" Amelia said. "I can tell you what I know but someone needs to fill in the rest. I have wondered for a long time if the hotel room, now your office, might hold some clues as well. The police back then didn't bother to check things thoroughly. You have the ability to find out the truth now."

Meghan was rendered speechless. She had to admit to herself that something had piqued her interest when she read the first article about the school's president and the investigator. She couldn't pinpoint why a seemingly innocuous mention in an 80-year-old newspaper held her interest but something–or someone, perhaps this Harrison Parker, whose name kept popping up in her life–wanted her to know about it.

"Well, I, uh, sure, I could try to help piece some of the information together," Meghan said. "But it's been 80 years. What could I possibly discover now that wasn't detected back then? And why didn't the local authorities do anything about it?"

"I know that Harrison had solved the mystery about my husband because he told me as much," Amelia said. "The problem is, he was killed before he could share with me–or his detective partner–what it was that he had discovered. His partner tried to piece it together but he was such a wreck after Harrison died that he could barely get past the grief, let alone investigate, because his boss and the police chief here stonewalled him anytime he tried. The local authorities were a joke at the time. They could have cared less that a police officer from another town who had invaded their territory uninvited had been killed. They closed the case saying that he shot himself accidentally. I don't believe it. I never have."

"Well, why don't you tell me a little more about your theory and I'll see if I can do some other research as well," Meghan said.

Amelia said she was getting tired and asked if Meghan could return the next day after lunch so they could discuss the matter further. Meghan agreed.

"Could you be a dear and kindly escort Emma and me back to our room?" Amelia asked.

Meghan gladly obliged but then asked, "Emma?" It was the first time she had heard the roommate's name.

"Yes, Emma here is my former husband, James Thornton's, daughter," Amelia said. "It's a very, very long story but she helped me when he tried to destroy my school and we became lifelong friends after he vanished."

As they turned to go back inside, Meghan noticed the garden again. It held stark white gardenias along with a colorful display of sweet peas and rose bushes. All were in full bloom.

"What kind of flowers are those?" Meghan asked. "They are exquisite."

"Oh, the white ones are gardenias. They indeed are exquisite," Amelia said. "The ones in different colors are sweet peas. The plants that are creating these flowers are 80 years old, my dear. I helped plant them myself. Harrison's daughter came to be a student at my school and we planted them as a way to honor her parents. Her mother, Madeline, adored gardenias, and her father nicknamed her

Sweet Pea. They served as a daily reminder to Penelope of her parents' love."

"She was such a sweet little girl and it was so heartwarming to always see her tending to the flowers," Emma chimed in. "She nurtured them and cared for them each day. It was a great testament to her love for her parents, even though they weren't here anymore. She had them here in spirit."

Meghan's head was spinning after she left the women. She had expected to learn something about a little old lady who had lived a long, prosperous and healthy life. And nothing more.

But this news was more than she ever imagined. She already had been enraptured with the Harrison-Thornton story. Now, she was completely captivated and had an odd desire to solve this mystery that existed in the town for the past 80 years. But she had no idea why she had been chosen to do so, or even how she would go about it.

CHAPTER 38

The next day, Meghan was called into the editor's office. The publisher was there as well. It was never a good sign to be called to a meeting with one or both of them on their territory. If they came to see her in her office, it was a mere nuisance matter; to be called to their turf was not a good thing.

Much to her surprise, the meeting started out somewhat OK.

"This Ross Perot fella is making a big deal about the economy," her editor, Alex Kingstone said. "I don't know if he has a real shot at the presidency but his message seems to be resonating with the voters. We want you to see if you can get an official statement from his campaign. But then we want you to contact the Bush/Quayle campaign and the Clinton/Gore campaign to get reactions from them about what Perot is saying. I'm sure they must have something to say about this quirky guy who is dominating the campaign right now."

Meghan contemplated how to answer without sounding negative. It always amused her that Kingstone thought they were a newspaper like the *New York Times* or the *Washington Post*, when in fact they were a community newspaper. It was a small town that people rarely heard of and their mission had always been to report the local news. Yes, they sometimes took global issues and melded them down to show relevance on the local level. But getting three presidential candidates to comment to her, an unknown reporter, was going to be a challenge.

"Well, we're a small town newspaper with not a lot of clout but I'll see what I can do," Meghan said. "If I can't get all three campaigns to talk to me, would it be OK if I tried to just do a 'man on the street' piece and ask what our local voters think about all three of the candidates' positions on the matter? Even if I can get the campaigns to give me a statement, I think we still should pick the brains of our local residents, too. Wouldn't you agree?"

Both nodded in agreement. Meghan silently complimented herself for putting the P.R. part of her degree to good use.

"That was easy," Meghan thought to herself, ready to get up and return to the matters waiting in her office. Then realized she thought too soon.

"On another matter, why were you snooping around Mercy Angels yesterday?" Kingstone asked gruffly, trying to show his command of authority in front of the boss.

"I wasn't snooping," Meghan said.

"What were you doing there?!?" Kingstone demanded.

"Following up on a story," Meghan said, still unshaken and not willing to reveal anything.

She found it difficult to take her editor seriously. He lacked height – she towered over him by at least 4 inches–and he was plump and egotistical. He also had no idea what he was doing.

"What story? You have been told to stay away from investigating anything there. We just discussed this last week and you now have the nerve to show up there and flaunt it in our faces?" Kingstone asked.

"You need to get a grip," Meghan said, looking at the publisher, who so far had not uttered one word. "I'm simply working on a follow-up story that I did several years ago, checking in on a sweet little old lady. Nothing sinister about it. You can report that back to your pals who are leaning on you to find out what I am up to. May I go now? I have a lot of work to do and these meetings are becoming tiresome and pointless."

Meghan usually didn't speak out like that to the bosses but she was getting tired of their shenanigans and was tired of defending herself.

Meghan headed back to her office and slammed the door.

"Of course I'm up to something, but now I'm going to need to be more discreet about it," Meghan told herself. "I wish my former editor was still here...Think, think, think. What would he do? How would he handle all of this nonsense?"

Some of her more friendly co-workers tapped softly on her door that afternoon, just to check on her and see if she was OK. They all were stunned that she had spoken up to the editor and had the guts to do what they had not.

While in her self-imposed hibernation, Meghan decided she would need to look for clues in her office, but she would have to do it when nobody else was around.

She also needed to call her friend Nick Gravinski, the investigator who always helped her when she got stuck on an investigation. The problem was, he was going to think she had hit her head or something when she outlined the story for him. He was a skeptic when it came to paranormal activity so he wasn't going to understand *this* one.

Before calling him, though, she called Rebecca, the activities director at Mercy Angels. Meghan asked if it would be physically possible to have Amelia and Emma meet her off-site. Given her conversation with the higher-ups, she decided it might be best to not appear back at the home for a while. Rebecca readily agreed and said it would be no problem. Rebecca said the ladies always enjoyed the chance to get some fresh air so they arranged to meet at the south end of the park that runs adjacent to the riverfront at 1:30 p.m. the next day.

CHAPTER 39

The next day, Meghan went to Mug's Pub for lunch, partly for the food but also to see if she could summon the "ghosts." She knew how ridiculous a thought it was to seriously believe she could summon anyone, but then again, they found her. Why couldn't she find them in this old, dark place? Maybe the place's history, if she ever learned it, would give her some inspiration.

The ghosts didn't appear.

After lunch, she had some time so strolled down along the river before heading to the park to meet Amelia, Emma and Rebecca. She could hear the calliope of the excursion boat that was rambling somewhere down south along the river.

Meghan imagined what it was like back in the day, in Amelia's day, when it was a real entertainment vessel. The boat was alive with music, dining and dancing. Old photographs showed men in suits and top hats, ladies at their sides in long flowing gowns, decorative hats and white gloves carrying parasols and strolling along the deck. Today, it went out on hour-long excursions during the day, giving the short-term sailors a brief history of the area and the importance of the river for the growth of the town, bringing commerce and a stable economy to the area over the decades.

As Meghan approached the park, she saw Rebecca assisting the women out of the Mercy Angels shuttle van. She ran to catch up and help.

Amelia greeted Meghan with a warm smile, as did Emma, for the first time. Either Amelia had a talk with Emma or Rebecca's bubbly personality was contagious. Meghan was hesitant to bring the old ladies and their wheelchairs out to a park but Rebecca's ease in handling the situation showed Meghan she need not worry. Taking care of the women and entertaining them came naturally to Rebecca, distracting them with her pleasant talk and compliments while she navigated the heavy lifting and the rickety pathway with the wheelchairs.

Once the women were settled and Rebecca and Meghan were seated on a park bench adjacent to them, Rebecca asked, "Now you're sure you two are up for this and want to tell everything, to both of us? I can leave for a while."

"Oh yes, dear, we are ready to tell our story and you absolutely are staying. You are a believer so you definitely can stay," Amelia said as she handed the women their bottles of water.

Amelia took a sip and then said, "The *Titanic,* such a tragedy."

Rebecca and Meghan raised their eyebrows to each other but indulged the woman nonetheless. They were traveling 80 years back in time so if the *Titanic* helped her clear out the cobwebs, so be it.

"It was a different time, back in 1912," Amelia said. "Life was simpler then. I feel nostalgic for that time period in a lot of ways. I must admit that a part of me liked the attitude of most men, the ones who were true gentlemen, and treated all of us like ladies. They respected us and took care of us. At least the good ones did. Life was simplistic, at least compared to now. We hadn't yet gone through the tumultuous times that the First World War and Second World War and the Vietnam War brought to our country. It's difficult to explain but life was peaceful and pleasant and happy, for the most part."

Meghan and Rebecca let Amelia visit with the memories that had been recaptured in her mind for a moment.

"But it also was a difficult time, particularly for women like us, who wanted to do more with our lives and help others along the way," Amelia continued. "But women only had four basic career choices back then: wife and mother, secretary, teacher, and a woman of not so respectful doings. Women who raised a ruckus, showed they had a brain or otherwise displayed a grasp of important things that affect the world were frowned upon. I didn't care about that and even sat on the town's civic board for a while, although I wasn't allowed to be elected because women didn't even have the right to vote yet, let alone be elected to a public servant position."

Meghan and Rebecca smiled and waited patiently as the old lady rambled.

"I chose teaching," Amelia said. "It was my passion to teach others and to some extent remains my passion still today, at this very ripe old age. I had owned my own school for four years before I got married. I built it on my own with a lot of hard work and resilience. Then I chose the wrong man and he tried to tumble my empire. He almost took down this entire town."

"What do you mean?" Rebecca asked.

"Have you two young ladies ever wondered about the *Titanic*?" Amelia asked without answering the question, returning to her original line of thought.

Rebecca and Meghan had no idea what the *Titanic* had to do with the big mystery but then again, it had been the *Titanic* articles that made Meghan take note and then discovered this Detective Parker and eventually led her to the two old ladies. So they indulged the digression.

"I am totally intrigued and drawn to that tragedy for some unexplainable reason," Meghan acknowledged. "In fact, there is supposed to be an exhibit of some of the recent artifacts that have been recovered since they discovered the wreckage of the ship in 1985. I think it's coming to one of the nearby cities in a couple of months. Would you ladies like to go? I think I can arrange a press tour for all of us."

"That would be a lovely thing to do," Amelia said. "I was drawn to the ship as well, so powerful and mighty. The photographs of it were beautiful. I would love to see some of the treasures they have recovered from the bottom of the sea. Ah, it was supposed to be 'practically' unsinkable–just like us women, right?" and winked to all three in her audience.

"It was such a shock when it sank," Amelia said. "I still think about all those people who lost their lives that dark, cold night. I had read about the ship for months before it made its maiden voyage. I so envied the passengers embarking on their journey to America. I wanted to be one of those society women, dining in first class, enjoying the open air and the freshness of the open sea. In real life, I could never have made such a trip but I so envied the beautiful ladies of society traveling with their rich, handsome male companions."

Amelia seemed lost in a different era.

Then suddenly, to Meghan, she said, "You need to know a few things before we get deep into my own story, which came to a head smack dab in the middle of the tragedy of the *Titanic*."

Meghan and Rebecca smiled at each other.

"First, Emma here was my first husband's daughter," Amelia said. "He was a scoundrel and left her and her mother high and dry. I didn't know this at first. I married him and he soon became president of my school. But then when he started messing with me and my school, I started some detective work of my own, with a little help from some friends, and discovered he had an estranged daughter. It took me a while but I was able to contact her. It also took me a while to assess that I could trust her and that she could trust me but we ended up becoming confidants, lifelong confidants as a matter of fact."

Amelia paused to take a sip of water; Emma just smiled. Meghan noticed that Emma always seemed to defer to her elder, if it could be termed that with a separation of just five years.

"At the same time, I had been corresponding with my good friend Madeline, who I had grown up with. We went to finishing school and education school together," Amelia continued. "We were living in different places but kept our friendship going through our correspondence. Then suddenly, her letters were no longer coming to me. I had revealed a lot to her about my situation in my letters to her and I was having her send her letters to me care of the owner, Frank, at Mug's Pub, just up the street here."

Amelia pointed up toward Main Street. Meghan nodded and said "I know it well."

"No kidding? It's still there? I would love to see it sometime, just to see how much it has changed, or perhaps stayed the same," Amelia said.

"We'll take a field trip for lunch someday, when you are up to it, and go with Meghan, if that is OK," Rebecca said.

Meghan nodded in agreement.

"Anyway, I was having her send her letters to Frank and Robert down at the pub," Amelia said. "I would go down there once or twice a week to collect the letters. Then they suddenly stopped and I feared that somehow my husband had found out what was going on and intercepted them. Frank and Robert insisted that no such thing had occurred."

Amelia's facial expression turned somber then and tears formed in her eyes. Rebecca stepped in and said, "Perhaps this is a bad idea. Maybe we should go back now."

Amelia held her shaky hand up in protest and said, "No, no. I'm fine. Just a difficult part of the story. It's been such a long time. But it's all coming back so vividly."

A long pause followed. Rebecca and Meghan exchanged concerned looks but Amelia regained her composure and continued.

"About a year after the letters stopped, I was in dire straits with the school and didn't know what to do or where to turn," Amelia said. "There were things going on with the town's finances as well, and my husband was directly involved. Frank and Robert helped me navigate through some of it and offered tremendous support and friendship. But there was only so much they could do."

"Then, out of the blue, this Harrison and his partner, Cutter, show up," Amelia said. "Kind of an odd couple. One went by his first name, the other by his last. Harrison was confident and smooth; Cutter seemed defeated yet determined. Something was going on with him but I could never pinpoint it. We'll get to him in a minute, though. Anyway, these two young men showed up and were willing to help me without having even met me or knowing what they were getting into."

"How do these two fit into the picture?" Meghan asked when Amelia paused to take a breath.

"You see, Harrison was Madeline's husband," Amelia said. "Prior to that, I had never had the opportunity to meet him but when he arrived at the school, I felt like I already knew him because of Madeline's letters. Now, normally, two strange men showing up claiming to be investigators of some type would have made me suspicious. But I immediately trusted Harrison because of Madeline. And I trusted this Cutter fella because Harrison trusted him."

Amelia then proceeded to tell Harrison and Madeline's love story as told to her through Madeline's letters and through Harrison's telling of what happened to Madeline while she was pregnant with their second daughter.

Emma placed a hand on Amelia's.

During the pause, Meghan asked, "Where are these letters today?"

"I have no idea," Amelia said. "I had given Madeline's letters to Harrison. He also had all of the letters that I had sent to Madeline. After he died, Cutter said he could not find where Harrison had kept them; they never turned up in the hotel room, at Harrison's house or his in-laws' house. They just seemed to vanish when Harrison died. Cutter always thought the local authorities just took them and destroyed the evidence."

Another far-away look crossed her face.

Rebecca decided that was enough for the day. But she did agree to set up another time and place to continue the conversation. It was scheduled to rain the next day so the foursome agreed to have that lunch at Mug's Pub.

CHAPTER 40

Rebecca parked at the curb in front of Mug's Pub. Meghan was walking south on the cobblestones from *The Main Informer* to the pub. Her heels were clicking away, echoing throughout Main Street.

She hurried to help Rebecca disembark the women from the van. They were using walkers today, which surprised Meghan.

Rebecca noticed her puzzled look and said, "They insisted on walking into Mug's Pub of their own accord, or at least with some minor assistance. Stubborn women."

Meghan smiled. "I thought they were either bedridden or wheel-chair-bound, what a nice surprise," Meghan said.

Emma and Amelia looked at each other, Amelia said "Today's youth!" and the pair rolled their eyes.

The two women shuffled through the front door, shooing away Rebecca's and Meghan's proffered hands. They barely allowed the younger women to open the door for them.

The four sat down at a table near the front of the pub. Once they were situated, and Emma and Amelia took in the surroundings, both nearly passed out. Meghan and Rebecca noticed their white-as-a-ghost expressions and turned toward the bar to see what was so compelling.

When Amelia gained her composure, she said, “Sorry, but the man at the piano is the spitting image of Robert Woodson, and the man behind the bar is the spitting image of Frank Henderson, the former proprietor of Mug’s Pub. It can’t be them, of course, because if that’s the case, they found the fountain of youth 80 years ago. It’s uncanny how much they look like them, though.”

Emma scanned the remainder of the restaurant and said, “They’ve kept everything as it was, with a few more knickknacks and artifacts that they must have collected in the last 80 years.”

Frank’s look-a-like came around from behind the bar and greeted the women.

“Good afternoon Miss Meghan, nice to see you again,” he said.

“Good afternoon, Kevin, how are you?” Meghan said, looking at the two older ladies for a reaction. “These are my friends, Rebecca and her charges, Amelia and Emma. Excuse their lack of a voice but I do believe they may have seen a ghost or two.”

Kevin looked inquisitively from Meghan to the elderly women.

“I’m so sorry, young man, but you look like an exact replica of the former proprietor of this fine establishment, Frank Henderson,” Amelia said. “It’s uncanny how much you look like him. You must be a great grandson at the very least. And your piano player looks like Frank’s former piano player.”

Kevin smirked.

“Ah, yes, mademoiselle, Frank Henderson indeed was my great-grandfather. I am Kevin Henderson,” Kevin said. “I hope we can meet the expectations that my great-grandfather established many decades ago when he started this wonderful place. How about a nice refreshing drink to start, perhaps an appetizer?”

When their orders were placed and Amelia returned to the present, she started in on her mysterious story again, almost as if it had not been interrupted by the passing of a day.

“Harrison withheld it from me for a bit but finally told me he was receiving threats,” Amelia said. “When I realized this could get dangerous, I asked Harrison to stop his investigation and go back to his daughter. I couldn't have anything happen to him. I couldn't do that to Madeline or her child. Penelope already had suffered so much in losing her mother and her unknown sister; I couldn't bear it if something happened to her father as well."

"Why didn't he quit then?" Meghan said.

"His honor. He felt a sense of duty to help and protect me and my charges because of Madeline," Amelia said. "Don't get me wrong, he wanted to protect his daughter, too. He loved her more than words and would have moved mountains for her. But sometimes a man's calling involves more than just his family. He feels that if he steps up and helps others, helps his community and his world, he is protecting his own family in the process. In some ways, that is true. But when it becomes an obsession to fix someone else's worries, it becomes a problem for one's own family."

Amelia sighed.

"Anyway, I begged him to go back home, forget about me and live his quiet, private life and honor his late wife by showering his daughter with love," Amelia said. "He would have none of that. He said he couldn't live with himself if he didn't try to help his wife's best friend, that in doing so, he *was* honoring his wife and her memory as well as honoring his daughter by stepping up to help someone in need. It was difficult to argue with that but I didn't want the guilt."

"So what happened?" Meghan asked.

"He did go home, for a few days at a time," Amelia said. "He spent time with his daughter and pondered a solution to my problems. He did his regular job and spent every waking hour that he wasn't working with his daughter. But my situation nagged at his heart and he always came back."

"You knew he would," Meghan said.

"Yes, fortunately for me and unfortunately for him," Amelia said.

Meghan raised her eyebrows in an inquisitive manner.

"He checked back into The Brass Inn," Amelia said. "He came to see me and told me he had figured out some of it. He just needed to complete some of the puzzle pieces but the time away had given him some fresh perspective and although it might be the wrong decision, he needed to proceed. I asked him if it was dangerous for him to continue investigating and he said yes, but was unfazed. I told him to stop, that it wasn't worth it and I would survive. But he insisted. Then his partner, Cutter, found him dead in his room."

"How did he die?" Meghan said.

"Someone shot him," Amelia said. "Although that's not what was reported in the newspapers and the town gossip. They all said he accidentally shot himself. Nobody ever heard a gunshot during the time frame before his body was discovered and nobody ever saw anyone go in and out of his room."

"They never figured out who did it, or why?" Meghan said.

"No," Amelia said. "Harrison had told Cutter before he returned to Tirtmansic that he had discovered something, something big. He asked him to return to Tirtmansic as soon as possible. But Cutter didn't make it here in time; Harrison died before he could reveal whatever he had uncovered. And to this day, I cannot fathom what was so bad that it had to result in Harrison's death."

"What about Cutter? He couldn't solve it on his own?" Meghan asked.

"Like I said, he was difficult to pinpoint," Amelia said. "He already seemed defeated when I met him. When Harrison was killed, he was gone. You could see the hollowness when you looked into his eyes. Don't get me wrong. He tried to figure out what his partner had figured out. He knew the guy like a brother so knew how he thought, how he operated, how Harrison would have deduced a solution. But he either was so wrapped up in his own grief about his partner's death that he couldn't see beyond that, or he was so lost without his partner that he just couldn't carry on anymore. It was almost like Cutter had been the body and Harrison was the head and once the head was 'cut off,' so to speak, Cutter could no longer survive."

"What happened to Cutter?" Meghan said.

"Well, he hit the bottle and carried out his days as a police officer, and later became a private detective, although I'm not really sure that he ever did any real detecting," Amelia said. "He was never the same after Harrison died. He was sleep-walking through his life. He came to live here and visited us–Emma, Penelope and me–often. He was the consummate gentleman, old-fashioned and protective of us girls. But he was so hollow inside. He was going through the motions of life and never recovered. The one shining spot was the day he proudly–alcohol-free, mind you–walked Harrison and Madeline's daughter, Penelope, down the aisle, to her husband, Robert Woodson the Second."

"So he turned himself around," Rebecca interjected.

"Well, he did for the duration of all the wedding preparations and festivities," Amelia said, then shot a look to Emma. "Unfortunately, that night, he walked out of this very establishment and died of a heart attack, right there on the cobblestone street."

CHAPTER 41

Meghan made good on her promise to take Rebecca, Amelia and Emma to the press preview of the *Titanic* exhibit. The experience proved to be extremely moving for all four ladies, but mainly Amelia and Emma, who had lived in the era of the tragedy. As they traversed through the exhibit, Meghan took on the duties as tour guide, reading and relating some tidbits about the doomed ship and the exhibit.

The wreckage of the *Titanic* had been discovered 2 ½ miles below the surface of the Atlantic Ocean, resting on the ocean floor, on Sept. 1, 1985.*

In August 1987, Titanic Ventures Limited Partnership contracted with IFREMER, the French oceanographic research institute, to conduct approximately 60 days of research and recovery operations at the *Titanic* wreck site. The expedition team recovered approximately 1,800 objects in 23 dives.

(*RMS Titanic, Inc.,* later acquired all the assets and assumed all the liabilities of Titanic Ventures Limited Partnership. Then *RMS Titanic, Inc.,* and IFREMER conducted a second joint expedition to the *Titanic*'s wreck site with the French research and recovery ship

Nadir.)

Exhibits of the artifacts began traveling to various sites across the country in 1991.

"It is amazing to me how many of the pieces are still intact," Rebecca said. "They are breathtaking and eerie at the same time."

It was true, as some of the china dishes and other artifacts miraculously remained in one piece, given the impact of the sinking ship. The ladies observed numerous open bottles of wine with the cork tapped in and the original liquid remaining in the bottle, untouched by the ocean's water. Some of the crystal glasses and tea sets also remained intact.

Meghan continued dispelling information for the other women:

The artifact exhibits serve as a living history of what happened on that ill-fated journey of the *Titanic* and the loss of life. Because of the precise re-creation of parts of the ship, including the bedrooms and dining rooms, walking through the exhibition makes one feel like they are walking on sacred ground, among the ghosts of *Titanic*. Except for the crews of the expeditions to the site, this is the closest contact most people can achieve to that awe-inspiring fateful night on the frigid Atlantic Ocean.

Additionally, patrons of the exhibit are given "boarding passes" that serve as admission tickets to the exhibit. For that evening, Meghan became "Mrs. Edward Beane (Ethel Clark)," hailing from Norwich, England. Her ticket, No. 2908, served as an authentic way to walk back in time through the exhibit "in character" of someone who actually had traversed the mighty ship's corridors and inhabited the cabins for a couple of days.

The authenticity of the pass and the re-created sleeping quarters, dining facilities and the grand staircase in the exhibit gave Meghan a chill. She felt like she was walking among ghosts of the great shipwreck.

After viewing the exhibit, Meghan conducted her own research about Mr. and Mrs. Beane, just to satisfy her curiosity. The Beanes were listed as second-class passengers and had just been married in March of 1912. They were on their honeymoon and believed to be just one of 12 newlywed couples on the ship, and the only honeymooners to survive together.

However, surviving together was a misnomer, Meghan soon learned from old news clippings, as Mrs. Beane was placed on Life Boat No. 13. But because of the "women and children first" rule, Mr. Beane was prohibited from boarding the half-filled boat. Not to be dissuaded, Mr. Beane took matters into his own hands and simply dived off the ship into the frigid waters of the Atlantic Ocean.

Newspaper accounts say he swam for at least an hour searching for his bride before being pulled out of the water into a lifeboat. Reports are conflicting as to whether he was pulled onto No. 13, by the arms of his own bride, or, as written in other accounts, the couple was not reunited until the *Carthapia,* the ship that raced to rescue *Titanic* survivors, had docked in New York City.

In a newspaper interview in the 1930s, Ethel Beane said that they had saved for six years for their wedding, which had taken place in Norwich, and had stored $500 along with 65 wedding presents that went down with the ship.

"For years I didn't want to talk about it," Beane had told a newspaper reporter years after the tragedy. "Wherever we went, people pointed at us curiously, and made us aware that death had brushed us by. We must have been a mile away in the rowboat when the *Titanic* went down. We could hear the band playing and then just before the crash of sinking the anguished cries of those on board which was like one great human wail. It was years before I could forget that terrible scream."

***

Reports indicated that Ethel Clarke, 19 at the time of her voyage, had served as a maid in a Norwich household while Edward Beane, 32, had been in Rochester, New York, to secure work as a bricklayer before returning to England for the wedding ceremony. Newspaper accounts report that the couple had two sons during their marriage.

One thing was certain: The couple never sailed on the ocean again.

According to newspaper reports, Ethel Clarke Beane was born on

Nov. 15, 1892, in England, and died on Sept. 17, 1983, in a nursing home in Rochester, N.Y., at the age of 90. Edward Beane was born on Nov. 19, 1879, in England, and died on Oct. 24, 1948, also in Rochester, N.Y. The cause of death for both was listed as heart failure.

Meghan realized that if Mrs. Beane, the character that she had become for the exhibit, had lived, she would have celebrated her 100th birthday this year, in November of 1992. She was the same age as Emma Thornton.

The fact that Edward Beane was a bricklayer also made Meghan ponder the cobblestone-laden Main Street that she traversed each day. She wondered who might have been the bricklayer of the street that seemingly liked to eat the heels of her shoes.

---

* Information about *Titanic* exhibits is from *RMS Titanic, Inc.* (rmstitanic.net). Personal information about Ethel and Edward Beane is gleaned from passenger lists, several articles, including those that appeared in the New York Times and other newspapers during their lifetimes.

***Rochester Democrat and Chronicle,* April 15, 1931.

CHAPTER 42

Meghan was working late one stormy night. The building was empty save for one or two other late-night stragglers working downstairs.

She picked up her fake boarding pass from the *Titanic* exhibit and pondered once again about the miracle of Edward and Ethel Beane. She thought again how ironic it was that he had been a bricklayer because much of Tirtmansic's Main Street was constructed of brick, from the cobblestone street to many of the buildings, built one brick at a time. She thought about what a painstakingly difficult job it must be.

Most of the walls inside *The Main Informer* displayed that same brick handiwork. Curiously, the walls of Meghan's office were covered in drywall and painted a dull white. She believed at one point that they had been bright white, but decades of newsprint had coated the walls with a dirty hue.

She wandered around the building and became even more curious. The exterior wall in her office was the only one that had drywall instead of exposed brick.

The next day, she called Diane at the Tirtmansic Historical Society to see if she could locate the original blueprints for the building and any building plans showing renovations over the years.

When she had the plans in her possession, she discovered that the building had been in existence at least since 1855 and at various times had served as a boarding house, hotel, grocer, restaurant or some combination of all four. In the 1950s, it became the office space for *The Main Informer*. Historical documents indicated that it once had been a first class hotel with impeccable hospitality and was considered one of the most thriving establishments of its kind in the region.

It had been a hotel when a cyclone struck the building in 1902 and one side of the building, the part where her office was located, had to be reconstructed. The original plans showed that there was a fireplace in that room at one time but when the hotel was renovated, the construction workers apparently just bricked in the entire wall, hiding the fireplace.

When the building was renovated for offices, someone apparently didn't appreciate the beauty of the brick so put drywall up all the way around the exterior walls. There didn't seem to be any documentation of when or why someone eventually tore down all that drywall to expose the original brick again. It was odd that the drywall had remained intact in her office.

At that moment, Pink Floyd's "*The Wall*" emanated from her radio, and Meghan heard the familiar refrain to "tear down the wall."

She stared at the wall in her office, then walked over to it. She poked at various places and after a few well-placed nudges, part of the wall gave way, white dust speckles blanketing her hand. She poked a little more and reached her hand into the hole.

Her fingers glossed over brick. She called Nick Gravinski, her detective friend and really her only male companion these days, to come over right away.

"Bring a sledgehammer," Meghan told him.

Nick arrived and started knocking down the drywall. Meghan admired the handiwork that someone, once upon a time, had diligently performed to create the structure. She ran her hand across the aged brick and felt some of the natural cracks that had formed over time. It had been hidden for 40 years so it didn't appear as aged as the other brick in the building.

Halfway up the wall, she felt something odd, a different kind of crack, an intentional crack.

She felt along the crack and at one point she thought a brick shifted on its own. She tried again and then Nick gave it a try. With a little more effort, he was able to pull the brick out completely. They pried a few more bricks loose and part of the wall finally gave way.

Meghan was met with the framed faces of a young family in an old-fashioned black and white image. There was the handsome young man seated next to his beautiful, young pregnant wife, his arm lingering around her shoulder. A cute little girl with curly hair stood between the couple with a toothless smile.

Meghan stared at the family smiling back at her and finally picked up the picture frame. She discovered it sat upon a pile of letters and a notebook. She recognized the man instantly. It was Harrison. But how did she know it was Harrison? She had never met him, she had only visualized in her own mind what he would look like.

After staring at the photo, Meghan looked down at the letters and what looked like a journal. Although she already had tainted the picture frame, before she pulled anything else out of its hiding place, Nick donned a pair of gloves and gave a pair to Meghan.

Although it was 80 years old, he said there might be traces of evidence on the items.

Nick used Meghan's phone to call in a favor to one of his buddies at the police department. They would put a rush on examining the evidence at the crime lab.

"I think we also need the lab to come and check your office for any evidence," Nick said.

"It has been 80 years, don't you think all traces of a crime are gone now?" Meghan said. "And if Harrison hid these here, and nobody else knew they were here, won't they only have his fingerprints on them?"

"You never know, with modern technology," Nick said. "We might find something that has survived all these years."

"The boss isn't going to like this," Meghan said, suddenly realizing what a mess they had made of her office. "He's going to wonder what the heck happened here and then he's not going to like this if he finds out that I've entangled myself in an 80-year-old mystery. He wants today's news, not news of yesteryear."

"It will be fine," Nick said. "Just tell him that the police are investigating something and they needed access to the wall. Tell him to send the police department a bill for the damages."

Both laughed at that prospect.

Meghan trusted Nick but wanted access to the information in the letters and journal immediately. She didn't want it to leave her sight. But donning his police hat, Nick insisted that it had to go through forensic tests and he promised they would examine the documents together.

"Why don't you come with me down to the station? You can personally witness it being logged into evidence and then tomorrow, the lab will rush its results," Nick said. "Trust me, these guys will take care of it. They are professionals and they are discreet. Nobody will know what we are doing here until it's necessary to clue others in."

***

When the documents were released back to Nick and Meghan, they sat in his closed office on South Main Street and pored over the hidden treasure.

The first one was curious to them, a plain ivory card with just the following written on it: "I know who you are and why you are here. Go away. Your work is done here. Thornton's dead." It clearly was a man's handwriting.

Next came the letters that Amelia and Madeline had exchanged over the years. They could feel Amelia's distress jumping off the delicate pages. They also could feel the warmth that Madeline exuded in encouraging and supporting her friend. The letters mostly just confirmed, in vague terms, what Amelia had already told Meghan.

They then turned their attention to Harrison's journal. He had been documenting every aspect of the investigation, down to the physical attributes of the hotel, Mug's Pub and every other place he had visited when he arrived in town in April of 1912. He had started with questions, a list of suspects, a list of people to interview who may or may not be suspects and the like. His list of suspects had nothing to do with a murder, at first.

One entry noted a letter that he had written to Penelope. They had not found that among the stash of letters exchanged between Amelia and Madeline.

"So where is that letter now?" Meghan asked. "Could it have been a final note dashed off to his daughter before he supposedly killed himself? And why did he even make a notation that he had written a letter to his daughter?"

Nick shrugged, focused on something else in the journal.

There was a notation about Robert Woodson keeping some sort of journal about the comings and goings in Tirtmansic at the time.

"Where is that journal now?" Meghan asked.

When they had read through the detailed notes and found themselves on the last page that was written in Harrison's writing, Nick and Meghan looked up at each other with wide eyes. They were astonished at what they had read, Harrison's conclusions about the original investigation and other things going on in the town.

Nick said simply, "Let's go talk to Amelia and Emma. Can you get that arranged for sometime this week?"

Meghan nodded and used Nick's phone to call Rebecca to set up a time and place. When she hung up, Nick said, "Let's get on the same page here. We don't want to reveal everything right away."

Meghan nodded in agreement.

"So we'll outline what we know, starting with the letters, but let's not mention the journal just yet," Nick said. "We can mention some of the theories listed in the journal but let's only reveal enough to try to jog their memories."

CHAPTER 43

Before meeting with Amelia and Emma again, Meghan and Nick began developing their own theories based on the evidence that they gleaned from the police reports, old newspaper articles, photographs and physical evidence. There really wasn't much physical evidence, however.

Nick had searched the Tirtmansic Police Department's archives and found the old police report, along with some of the evidence.

"You won't believe this but there's a storage box of evidence related to the case still intact in the basement evidence locker of the police station," Nick told Meghan when he found it.

However, the evidence and the police report didn't contain a lot of details. It mostly included documentation about what was found in the hotel room: normal hotel room accessories such as the bed, a desk and chair, along with Harrison's possessions found on his body, including a wallet full of cash, a scrunched pack of cigarettes, matches with Mug's Pub listed on them, keys and the key to the hotel room.

The report contained black and white photographs that were

taken of the crime scene, some with the body lying on the floor, others minus the body but the taped outline marking where the body had once lain. Nick stared at the photos for several hours, looking for clues.

He noted that Harrison's gun was placed in an odd position. He supposedly was shot in the chest but the way the gun was positioned in his hand, it wasn't aimed at his chest. In fact, it was aimed behind him, toward the window. The gun also was placed in his left hand.

He wondered if Harrison was right-handed or left-handed. He made a note to ask Amelia and Emma that question.

Nick requisitioned any documents that Police Sgt. Lance Cutter may have had. There was a brief item in the official police report in which Cutter had expressed skepticism about Harrison shooting himself and detailed why.

The interview with Harrison's in-laws stated that Harrison was despondent but based on the story that Amelia and Emma had told about Harrison's love for his family and especially the daughter who had lost her mother suddenly and tragically when she was only 6 years old, Nick was inclined to lean toward Cutter's thoughts instead of the Tirtmansic Police Department's conclusions. Nick suddenly was embarrassed to be affiliated with the Tirtmansic Police Department.

He had witnessed similar sloppy police work during his time here, too, though, so he wasn't at all surprised.

The report stated that two bullets were missing from Harrison's gun chamber. The official assumption was that Harrison had killed the now-missing Thornton and disposed of his body somewhere and that the second bullet had killed Harrison. Some police officers surmised that he was doing his wife's dear friend a favor in knocking off her husband, and then his guilt had gotten the better of him for killing a man in cold blood, so he offed himself.

But Nick wondered, "Did they ever test his gun to see if it had been fired, or had Harrison simply not filled the entire chamber?"

Harrison's gun was in the evidence container so he requested a ballistics test on it to see if it would provide any further evidence.

There was no suicide note, although Harrison supposedly wrote a note to his daughter.

"I doubt a father would write a suicide note to his 6-year-old daughter," Nick said.

***

Meghan went back to Mug's Pub and inquired of Kevin Henderson and his piano man, Jonathan Woodson. She learned that Harrison's daughter, Penelope, had married Robert the First's son. She wondered if Jonathan Woodson, the great-grandson of Robert Woodson, might have some old documents somewhere, including the journal that Robert supposedly had kept. She also inquired about a letter or any other correspondence that Harrison might have had with his daughter, Penelope, before his death.

Jonathan said he remembered hearing about some journals that his great-grandfather had kept and promised to try and locate them.

After Meghan and Nick compiled all the police information and Harrison's documentation, they started creating a list of potential suspects regarding Thornton's disappearance or death as well as Harrison's death.

They included everyone, even if they believed the people to be innocent: Amelia, Emma, Robert, Frank, government officials at the time. They thought that perhaps Thornton had killed Harrison and left town. They had not come to any substantial conclusions yet.

They needed more information from Amelia and Emma. They also needed to read Robert Woodson's journal.

CHAPTER 44

"Did you know that Robert Woodson was a private investigator?" Meghan asked Amelia and Emma.

Both women looked at each other. Meghan and Nick couldn't decipher their emotions.

"I had no idea, did you?" Emma asked Amelia.

"Well, no, I had no idea he was a private investigator," Amelia said. "It makes sense, though. He always knew a lot of things about what was going on in town. He had been playing that piano at Mug's Pub, I think, since Frank and his wife opened the restaurant in 1901. I just assumed that it was because he played that piano and had a way of weaseling things out of people while they were enjoying their spirits. I didn't know he had this other secret life. But I guess that explains a lot of things about him. He always wanted to investigate things but never was the one who got out in front of it. He manipulated someone else to be the front person. Interesting."

"Harrison wrote in his journal that Madeline had hired Robert to keep an eye on things after you started sending letters to her," Meghan said. "He had found payments to Robert among his wife's things."

"What journal?" Emma asked.

"The one he used to document every detail of his investigation while he was here, and then some," Nick responded.

"So Harrison knew all along when he came here that Robert was a private investigator, too?" Amelia asked.

"Apparently," Nick chimed in. "He wrote that after being in Tirtmansic for a couple of weeks, he finally revealed himself to Robert and the two started collaborating on information. It was not a coincidence that one of the first places Harrison visited when he came to town was Mug's Pub, and that he returned quite often."

"I wonder if Frank knew about Robert," Amelia said.

"He did, according to Harrison's journal," Nick said. "Frank hired him originally to be a piano player and then learned his secret and thought it provided his restaurant even more security to have someone keeping an eye on things in a covert manner."

Nick abruptly changed the subject and asked the women if Harrison was right-handed or left-handed. Both women were perplexed about the question but Amelia replied, "I'm not sure if I remember but you know, when he ate, I believe he used his right hand."

Emma sat in silence, never answering the question, just silently listening to everything that Meghan and Nick had come up with so far.

"Is it just me or does Emma look more and more frail and pale as the days go on?" Meghan asked Rebecca at one point during the debriefing sessions. Rebecca nodded in agreement.

After listening to the theories and storytelling for a few days, Emma declared that she had something to say. Emma had been sick with a fever and a nagging cough since the lunch at Mug's Pub. So Rebecca, Meghan, Nick and Amelia gathered around Emma's bed for this particular briefing.

"I am not sure where to start," Emma said, sounding weaker and with labored breathing. She looked at Amelia. "I never knew that you had been corresponding with Detective Harrison Parker's wife and that that was the reason he had come to town, because the voice in the letters had beckoned him. I never had any idea that that innocent-seeming piano player was really a private investigator. And I didn't know that Detective Parker had kept a journal documenting everything that was going on."

Nick cleared his throat. Emma continued.

"Well, I guess you already know or are going to figure it out in due time anyway, since you've figured out this much," Emma said.

She paused again. Then focused on Rebecca, thinking she might be the only friendly face in the room in a minute.

"I ... killed ... Harrison," Emma uttered.

Amelia gasped. All eyes darted back and forth between the two elderly women. Amelia's eyes revealed neither contempt nor surprise. In fact, they didn't reveal anything.

"It was an accident. I didn't have any intention of killing him," Emma continued, suddenly finding her voice. "I went to see him and I had been drinking and I went all crazy on him because he wouldn't tell me where the money was. I was positive he knew something or was part of my father's scheme because I had run into him several times. I grabbed my gun and it accidentally fired, straight through his heart apparently. He was dead instantly."

The reality started to sink in for all of them and Meghan looked at Amelia to gauge her expression. Something suddenly dawned on Amelia.

"But you were helping me and you helped save my school," Amelia said. "And oh my God, you helped me raise Harrison's daughter, knowing full well that you had deprived that poor, dear child of her own father."

Emma started crying then.

"I know, I know," Emma said. "I never meant for any of it to happen. It's such a long story and I've kept it a secret for so long. Only one other person ever knew, and that was my mother. I told her when she was on her deathbed. She had tried to take the blame for it and placed me in your care because she knew you would provide a better life for me."

"Please, do, go on. We have nothing but time to hear all of it,"

Nick, suddenly said, cutting through all the female-induced emotion in the room.

Meghan looked at Nick and thought back to their earlier conversation about the implications and potential punishment of a 100-year-old woman who committed a murder 80 years ago that had long been forgotten.

"I, uh, can you please leave?" Emma asked Nick.

"Sorry, but I'm staying right here, and I intend to witness the unraveling of this whole charade for myself," Nick said. "Proceed."

Emma sighed and said, "Well I suppose it doesn't matter now what happens to me."

Nick shot her a look as if to say he was losing his patience.

"My mother told me, also on her deathbed, that she knew who killed my father and your husband, James Thornton," Emma said, staring intently at Amelia. "Dad snookered her somehow and took all of her money, too. When you reached out to me for help to swindle him and get him back at his own game, I happily obliged. I was 20 years old and had nothing. My own mother and father had never paid much attention to me. I was a distraction and nuisance to them. They treated me like I didn't even exist. My mother tried but she wasn't capable of raising a child on her own. I saw an opportunity to help you, double-cross my father and thought I'd wind up with all the money from both the brothel and your school. Then I could go make my own life and be rid of everyone forever."

Amelia was too shocked to speak.

"In the beginning, I really was playing both sides," Emma said. "Then I got to know you and Frank and Robert. I finally realized that some people actually believed in me. I discovered what a kind, warm-hearted woman you are and I saw how much you loved the girls, as if they were your own children. And you took an interest in me. Nobody had ever done that. But you were willing to teach me how to read and write and gave me an opportunity to influence other people. I tried to push you away but you were pretty persistent. So I planned to get your part of the money back and give it to you–or at least most of it. Then I was going to take the rest and just disappear, start a new life and live happily ever after, as they say. I got greedy and I knew Thornton had the cash somewhere. I just couldn't ever find it. Then he came back."

"Who came back?" Amelia asked.

"James...Thornton....your husband.....my father," Emma said.

Amelia started at Emma. When she could speak, all she could muster was "When?"

"Remember when Mug's Pub was set on fire?"

Amelia nodded.

"That was him, he set fire to the place," Emma said.

"How do you know this?" Amelia asked.

Emma paused a long time. Then said, "I kept seeing him around town. I thought it was a ghost or my imagination for the longest time. Then I realized he really was here and made contact with him under the premise that I still wanted my cut of the money. I really was going to try to get it back so I give it to you, to pay you back for everything that you had done for me. Also as a way to make amends to Penelope for losing her father at my hands."

"So what happened to him and the money?" Nick chimed in, starting to become impatient.

"I don't know," Emma said. "I followed him to the tunnels so assumed it was there somewhere."

"What tunnels?" Meghan asked.

"There are tunnels that lead from the school property, well, now the nursing home property, down to underneath Main Street," Emma said. "Legend has it that they were used during the Civil War. I don't know if they still are there or even accessible anymore."

"Where is the entranceway on Main Street?" Meghan asked.

Emma looked back and forth between Meghan and Nick and then said, "Underneath Mug's Pub and some other buildings, including *The Main Informer,* but they led into the basement of the hotel that occupied that space at the time. I figured out that my father was getting ready to flee, and he was going to leave me high and dry. He had the look of someone desperate to escape so I followed him one night and discovered him going to the tunnels. I surprised him the night before his intended departure and discovered that he had a kind of shelter down there, with supplies and everything. He had a bag packed, ready to go. I pulled my gun on him and demanded the cash. He said he didn't have it with him, but he would have it the next night and if I didn't tell anyone, I could go with him and share the loot."

"And you believed he'd be there the next night?" Nick scowled.

"He was there the next night," Emma said. "But he didn't have the cash with him. I demanded to know where it was. He said he had it carefully hidden where nobody would ever find it. He then proceeded to taunt me and tell me that I was just as useless and clueless as my mother and Amelia and that he in fact was not going to give me a cut of the cash."

"So what happened at this point?" Nick asked.

"Someone had followed one or both of us down into the tunnels," Emma said. "I didn't know who it was because it was dark but somehow their aim was perfect. They took a shot and he fell over. I assumed he was shot in the back. Then I fled. I wasn't going to be shot, too. I panicked and ran in the opposite direction of the gun shots, straight back to the hotel. I went to my room, changed clothes and went down to Mug's Pub, where I proceeded to drink more than I should. I ended up sharing what happened with Frank and Robert. They told me they would take care of things."

"What did that mean?" Nick asked.

"I wasn't sure and didn't inquire at the time," Emma said. "A few days later, they told me they had gone down to the tunnels and didn't find a body but did find traces of blood. They thought that maybe my father had escaped or someone had dragged him out of there."

"So why didn't whoever was down there with you try to follow you and shoot you, too?" Nick asked.

"They might have tried but I guess they were more interested in my father than me," Emma said. "I don't even know if they saw me but I imagine if they stood there long enough, they at least would have heard my voice and what we were discussing. I did look over my shoulder for several years after that, always scrutinizing people in town and wondering if it was someone I knew."

"So you knew Thornton was dead or gone and supposedly not ever returning. Again, why did you go to see Harrison and kill him?" Nick said.

Tears formed at the edges of Emma's eyes again.

Emma took a deep breath and asked Rebecca for a sip of water, which took a painstakingly long time for her to manage. Finally she sighed and continued.

"Harrison came into Mug's Pub one night and sat at the end of the bar, where he had become a regular fixture during his brief stay here," Emma said. "He was having dinner and a couple of drinks. Then he went back to his room. I waited 10 minutes before I went back to the hotel. I took a chance that that's where he had gone and knocked at room 212.

"He opened the door and ever the gentleman, did not invite me in. But I walked in anyway. I had bought a bottle of scotch and two shot glasses so filled each one to share."

Emma explained that she just wanted to know where the cash was and had overheard him tell Amelia that he had solved most of the puzzle.

"I asked him what he knew. He told me that he had solved the mystery and wanted to talk to Amelia first," Emma said. "He said he couldn't tell me where the cash was located. I asked about his partner, Cutter. Where was he? What did he know? Someone had to know something. 'He doesn't know anything. I haven't had a chance to talk to him or anyone else yet but I will,' " Harrison had told me. "By this point, after a couple of shots, on top of what I already had been drinking at the bar, I got angry and upset. I pulled my gun on him and accidentally shot him."

Emma stopped for a minute, then started sobbing.

"I didn't mean to kill him," Emma said. "I really didn't. I am so sorry, Amelia."

"How did you get out of the room without anyone noticing?" Nick asked. "Didn't anyone hear the gun shot?"

Emma said that the second floor of The Brass Inn was mostly unoccupied at the time and explained that she had hastily cleaned up the place and arranged Harrison's gun in his hand so it looked like he shot himself. She said she tried to make sure none of her fingerprints were left in the room. She thought her prints were only on the bottle of scotch and the two glasses as well as the door knob.

"I grabbed the bottle and glasses and left through the back door of the hotel. I didn't want to risk going through the tunnels," Emma said. "I then walked around Main Street for a bit, so people could be witnesses to the fact that they had seen me out and nowhere near the hotel. Then I walked back into the hotel through the front door, made sure the hotel clerk and others saw my arrival and went upstairs to my guest room."

"What ever happened to the bottle of scotch, the two glasses and your gun?" Nick said.

"I wiped them down and tossed them all in the river," Emma said. "The gun wasn't mine to begin with. I had stolen it from the brothel. The women there had guns that were used in case a customer got out of hand. They never really shot anyone, as far as I know, but it was effective when one of the women needed to pull it on an aggressive patron. My intent was the same. I never planned to use it as a weapon, just as a threat to get what I wanted from my father."

Nick returned to his original line of questioning.

"Who shot Thornton, Emma?" Nick asked first.

"I don't know," Emma said.

"That's a convenient answer. Plausible deniability. Nobody saw you and nobody knows you were involved except Frank and Robert and your mother. And they're all dead," Nick said. "But as far as we know, you were the last person to ever see the man alive. You shot Harrison. That means you were capable of shooting Thornton, and even dragging him out to dump him in the river, too."

"But I didn't," Emma said. "I did kill Harrison, accidentally, but I absolutely did not kill my father. Someone else did that."

"Who, Emma?" Nick asked. "Who was in the tunnels with you that night? You know who was there?"

Emma looked back and forth to the three pairs of eyes staring at her. She finally spoke. Quietly.

"It was Detective Cutter," Emma said.

Amelia gasped. "What?" she asked.

"I didn't know it at the time," Emma said. "I found out at Penelope's wedding. I told him everything I had done and that my Dad had returned and was responsible for the fire and that I was ready to face the consequences. He then admitted to me that he had figured all of that out, and that in fact, he was the one who had followed us to the tunnels that night and shot Thornton to put all of us out of our misery, and to avenge Harrison's death. Ultimately, he felt it was James Thornton who had killed Harrison, even though I was the one who had pulled the trigger. He was trying to protect all of us and put an end to all the torment and anguish."

"And then he died that night out on the street," Amelia said.

Emma nodded.

"Yes, it was like he had made his confession and his work here was done," Emma said. "I pondered telling you all of this after Detective Cutter died but then I realized that all of us had been set free. Except the money now was gone forever. None of us had to live with all the anxiety, waiting for the next bad thing to happen. And I decided to try to make amends, which I've been trying to do, for the rest of my life, by helping you and Penelope and Frank and Robert and their children..."

Emma's voice trailed off as a flood of tears overwhelmed her.

After a long pause, Amelia finally asked "What *did* happen to all of the money? It has to be somewhere."

"I spent a number of years trying to find the cash, to give it back to you, Amelia," Emma said. "I had planned to anonymously get it back to you, but we could never find it. All those times you asked Robert to search the grounds because you thought someone was lurking behind the trees. That was me. I was going into the tunnels that run from Main Street to the school trying desperately to find the money. I know it has to be buried down there somewhere but I could never find it."

"Harrison had discovered where it was," Meghan said.

Emma's eyes flew open wide.

"What? He denied knowing anything," Emma said.

"He might have denied it but he had figured out where it was," Meghan said. "He just never got the chance to tell anyone, obviously, because he was waiting for his partner to return to retrieve it. And you said he wanted to talk to Amelia first. But you killed him and the secret died with him. That is, until his journal detailing his investigation was discovered, just days ago."

CHAPTER 45

Thornton had stashed the cash, literally, under the cobblestones. And it was more than the $2 million that he had told Emma he had hidden.

Harrison had noted in his journal entries that he could see the cracks in the cobblestone street from his hotel room window. Before meeting with Amelia and Emma, Meghan and Nick had gone back to her office and looked out the window, the same vantage point where Harrison had stood 80 years earlier.

"Something is hiding in plain sight," Meghan said as she and Nick noticed the same elevation, or cracks, in the cobblestone formation, that Harrison had noticed.

"Don't call me crazy, but you know, I keep hearing someone's shoe nail tapping on the cobblestones every time I walk down Main Street, and my heels keep getting stuck in the cracks," Meghan said. "I thought the clicking sound was just my imagination, or an echo. But was that really Harrison's ghost trying to point me here?"

Nick just gave her a look. He still wasn't totally sold on the ghost theory despite everything that had transpired in the past few days.

Nick had called in his crime scene investigation squad and they quickly converged at the site. The team erected an "evidence gathering" tent and placed police crime scene tape around the area. This portion of Main Street was closed to through traffic several years earlier and it was a quiet Sunday afternoon so the scene barely caught anyone's attention.

The team started peeling up the cobblestones one at a time until they found a wooden door underneath. Once they pried that up, they discovered it led down to another set of tunnels.

There were rickety makeshift wood rung steps that clearly an amateur had nailed into the sides as a way to get up and down. Nick noticed to the right as he descended into the tunnels that there was a makeshift door and latch. He tried to undo the latch but would need a tool to pry that open as well. He hollered for someone to send down a crow bar.

When the door finally swung open on its rusty hinges, he saw stacks of more money than he'd ever seen in his lifetime.

"Evidence bags needed! Large! Now!" Nick hollered up the hole.

Nick climbed back up the shaft and told Meghan and the crime scene technicians what he had discovered. Nick continued down the hole and let the technicians gather the evidence out of the safe. Meghan wanted to come down, too, but because it now was an official crime scene, it was off limits to her.

Nick reported that it mostly was cobwebs and caked mud and water puddles. But he wanted to make sure the team combed through every nook and cranny for every possible type of evidence.

Before meeting with Amelia and Emma, Nick had an inventory of the tunnel's contents on his desk.

"I can't say for certain that it's Thornton's body but they did find what's left of skeletal remains," Nick told Meghan. "They also found a revolver. The remains and the gun have been sent to the lab for testing and analysis. Our best hope is that we can find dental records to match the remains and track down the owner of the gun. I don't know if we can confirm anything but it seems logical that if he stashed the cash down there, he may have died there."

"Let me know as soon as you know something," Meghan said, then added, "I am intrigued by this whole thing just because of the whole mystery of it. But Nick, even though this is all 'off-the-record' for the moment, the higher-ups are getting restless. They want a story. They usually don't care much about these types of stories but since we destroyed the wall in my office and the cobblestones have been peeled up in front of their building, they want to know what the heck is going on. I've been holding them at bay, telling them that it's an ongoing investigation and you guys can't release much information yet but when you do, we get the exclusive."

"Understood. I promise you will get all of the details the moment I know them. You will get the exclusive," Nick said before saying his good-byes and hanging up.

Nick had taken a solo trip down into the tunnels from the street access point and what Emma had said about them was confirmed.

When he headed east, to his right, he found an entranceway that led up to *The Main Informer*, which would have been The Brass Inn 80 years ago. When he headed west through the tunnels, he had quite a distance to cover, mostly in the dark save for his high-beam flashlight and a cramped cement-encased pathway. He found an occasional small room that indicated that the tunnels must have been used for shelter at some point.

The tunnel ended eventually at the Mercy Angels Nursing Home, although it appeared nobody had been using the tunnels for illicit activities inside the nursing home.

CHAPTER 46

Given Emma's revelations, Rebecca said she would have Emma moved immediately to a different wing of the nursing home but Amelia was the one who said "no" to the idea.

"Do you think she's going to kill me in the middle of the night?" Amelia asked. "Look at her. She's so frail and defeated. She can't even lift a finger. Just leave her be."

Rebecca reluctantly agreed and said, "If you need anything, you push the panic button, yell as loud as you can and call for security as soon as possible, you understand?"

Amelia just laughed and said, "Seriously, Miss Rebecca, don't worry about it. I've known this woman for 80 years. While what she did was wrong and she should have confessed a long time ago, the Emma I know would not harm a fly let alone me. Now go and worry about something that's important."

When they were alone, Amelia sat on the chair next to Emma. Emma just stared at her with an unsettled look.

"Relax, Emma," Amelia said. "I'm not going to hurt you. I just have a couple of questions. I took you under my wing when you were

20 because you needed stability and an education, and more importantly, someone to love you. I never suspected that you were involved in Harrison's death and if I had known back then, I don't know that I would have been as forgiving as I am now. And I am grateful that young Penelope never found out the truth, that her dearest friend was responsible for her father's death."

Tears formed anew in Emma's eyes, and Amelia started crying, too. Amelia took Emma's cold hand in hers and continued.

"You were a perfect student and you hung onto every lesson I taught you," Amelia said. "I was and still am very proud of what you made of your life after your rough start in this world. You were dealt a bad card when you were so young but you straightened up and became a beautiful, perfect lady."

Emma interrupted her.

"You don't have to do this," Emma said. "My original intent was to give you back what you were owed and then I was going to take off. Then I ended up really liking you, loving you. Even though you were only five years older than me, I looked at you as if you were my adopted mother. You have no idea how long I have wrestled with the guilt of all of this. I had been handed a second chance and I didn't want to lose that. As the years went by, it became harder and harder to tell you the truth. I was afraid I was going to lose the best thing that had ever happened to me."

Amelia tried to interrupt but Emma continued.

"I tried to make amends to you in my actions," Emma said. "I worked so hard to help you rebuild your school. Even though I wasn't the one who had wronged you, I felt like I needed to make amends on my father's behalf. Then I had to wrestle with the guilt of taking Harrison away from that beautiful daughter of his. Her presence at the school was almost like a constant penance for me and I realized that I favored her more than the other girls because of my guilt. It was my fault that she lost her father because I had a vendetta against mine. My heart ached for her every time I saw her but I loved her so much and would do anything for her. In a way, I am glad that she never knew the truth."

Amelia asked, "Why now?"

Emma managed a smile amidst the tears.

"I'm old, Amelia," Emma said. "Look at me. You're older than me but you're going to outlive me. My days are numbered and I know it. That reporter and her detective friend had a good story going there and I could have just left it that way. But they were going to figure it out. I think they might have already figured it out, they just wanted me to be the one to tell the story. It was time. I needed to tell you so you knew. I never intended for it to work that way and I have regretted it all of my life."

"No need to think about it anymore," Amelia said. "The past is the past and we can't change it, no matter how hard we try."

Emma started to say something but Amelia quieted her.

"We both have lived a good life, my child, and you should be quite proud of the lady you became despite how your life started. I know I am extremely proud of you for turning your life around, becoming a respectable lady and living a long, fulfilled life," Amelia said. "My hope is for you to rest in peace, my dear friend."

CHAPTER 47

Meghan turned in two stories to the editor at *The Main Informer*. The first one detailed the conclusions of the mystery that had transpired 80 years ago with Amelia and Emma. She figured not many people would care about that story as much as the other one. After all, it was the mystery of something that had happened so long ago. The most she could hope for is that the townsfolk would enjoy reading a nice little feature story that told a bit of the history of the town. It also detailed the connection of the former Annabelle Adams School for Young Ladies to the current Mercy Angels Nursing Home, and the fact that the woman whose namesake was on the school was now a resident in that very home, on the same property where her school once housed young ladies anxious to learn about the world.

However, the article revealed something no one had even considered back in 1912.

It turned out the body that had been found in the tunnel was not Thornton's. Instead, it was that of the police chief of Tirtmansic circa 1912, George Greyber. Forensic testing showed that the gun was police-issued and the crime scene investigators combed through dental records of law enforcement officials from that era.

But they pretty much had confirmation it was Chief Greyber already because of what was found with the body, what appeared to be a police report written by him, about his imminent death. The gun also could be traced back to him and one bullet was missing from the chamber.

The note indicated that Greyber had discovered Thornton's hiding place. The state police had showed up in town to investigate the police department, Greyber's department, and the kickbacks; the state police had forced the brothel to be shut down and according to the report, Greyber thought Thornton had double-crossed him.

He thought Thornton had reported him to the state authorities for having a corrupt police department. Greyber later decided he should have realized it couldn't have been Thornton because he would have gone down with the ship in a corruption investigation as well...unless Thornton somehow was paying off the state police, too.

Greyber thought that's why Detective Harrison Parker was in town, initially, to investigate the corrupt police department. But then Greyber realized he was investigating Thornton and so decided to turn the tables on Thornton.

Greyber had conducted surveillance on Thornton and discovered his secret passages into the tunnels. He went down one night and discovered Thornton talking to someone and then heard gun shots. Greyber knew he hadn't been seen so left via one of the offshoots of the tunnels. He intended to return to make sure Thornton was dead. But when he returned, there wasn't a body anywhere in sight.

The police chief already knew what Amelia and Woodson had not discovered until later: there was corruption at all levels of the local government and Thornton was at the center of all of it. Greyber had decided that he was going to put an end to all of it and take care of what he termed "this arrogant scumbag" once and for all, although he still wanted his cut. But then someone else had handled it for him, or at least made Thornton disappear. Still, Greyber knew he was finished.

"Greyber must have shot himself after writing the report, and his decaying body, along with the report, remained there hidden in the deep, dark tunnels for 80 years," Nick said.

However, Nick was skeptical about this new twist in the mystery, too. While Nick understood that Greyber might have been searching for the cash in the tunnels after Thornton was gone, there was something odd about finding the police report with his body. Nick couldn't figure out why a police chief would write an entire report and bring it down into a dark tunnel with him, indict himself in writing for the murder of James Thornton, and then kill himself, knowing that potentially the information would never be released to the public.

It was all too coincidental and seemed like it was more of a set-up by someone else. Another question that bothered Nick was, why hadn't anyone in Tirtmansic even noticed that the police chief had gone missing? Or did they? Another research mission loomed.

Nick found his answer among the archives of the police department, discovering a personnel file containing a document that was a written resignation from Greyber as Chief of Police. It stated that he was leaving town and from what Nick could deduce, he was never heard from again.

"But why does this look like a woman wrote the resignation letter," Nick said to Meghan when he showed it to her. "Look at how it has loops and flowery letters. And it doesn't match the handwriting on the police report."

Meghan yawned and said, "I'm tired. Let's look over this again when I can clear my head."

But she knew Nick would stay up all night trying to solve this new puzzle.

CHAPTER 48

While the article about the 80-year-old mystery contained intrigue, drama and suspense, Meghan felt her investigative story about Mercy Angels Nursing Home deserved more prominence in the newspaper. After all, it had more relevance to present-day issues.

She felt that the story was her piece de resistance, the air-tight investigation of the nursing home's owner.

With Rebecca's secret help, Meghan had uncovered the fact that the owner, Robin Richards, and the accountant, Alexandra, who happened to be Robin's wife, had been defrauding Medicaid for years, double-billing for patients and pocketing the extra money.

The nursing home's official books only showed the correct billing figures, thus nobody questioned where the extra funds were directed. But Meghan had a friend at the Tirtmansic Regional Bank, who could have lost her job for revealing the fact that the Richards had two bank accounts. One was for Mercy Angels Nursing Home's operating expenses. The other was listed as Mercy Angels Nursing Homes-private, and the funds were paying for a luxurious lifestyle of travel, fancy cars and three mansions, one in Tirtmansic and two on separate beaches in Tahiti and Puerto Rico.

The Richards also were skirting the tax laws by declaring the Mercy Angels Nursing Home as a charitable organization affiliated with a church. Religious organizations aren't required to pay the high taxes on property and income that other businesses are required to pay.

The Richards funneled their income to an offshore bank account to avoid paying their personal income taxes. In fact, the Richards reported a loss every year.

"How in the heck can someone have three mansions, two fancy cars and travel all over Europe while reporting a loss?" Meghan had asked Rebecca at the beginning of the investigation.

Meghan couldn't quote Rebecca directly but her insider tips led her to finding all the documentation that she needed to write a complete story. Meghan was able to get government officials to go on the record and they even launched an investigation of their own. As it turned out, the Richards owned five other similar nursing homes throughout the United States and were carrying out the same fraudulent schemes as they were at Mercy Angels.

When Meghan confronted the Richards with all of the documentation, Robin would not allow Alexandra to utter one word. Then he proceeded to lie through his teeth about what was going on.

"People who work for me are setting me up," Robin Richards had told her. "My wife oversees the accounting, of course, but she had no idea that the people who work for her were cooking the books and not paying the taxes as required. I will find out who is defrauding the government in my name and find out why the taxes seem to be in disarray. I will launch my own investigation and I will find out who is behind all of this. You can trust me on that. I will find out who is doing this to me and the matter will be corrected internally."

Meghan let Robin Richards rant and change the subject and deny, deny, deny knowledge of anything going on right under his nose.

"I intend to quote you as claiming you have no knowledge of what is going on in your own nursing home, which is quite frightening considering there are people who are relying on your good faith to take care of them," Meghan told him at the end of his rant. "And I am running the story as I presented it to you because the documentation tells the entire story. You cannot refute any of that. The readers will be able to figure out for themselves where the truth lies."

***

Meghan couldn't believe what she was hearing. The publisher of *The Main Informer* had almost no interest in the little mystery story but was convinced enough that people love to read historical facts about their town to let it be published. But he flat out was refusing to publish the well-researched, well-documented article about the fraud and criminal activities going on at the nursing home.

In Meghan's eyes, the fraud and criminal activities had a much larger and broader impact on the readers. It involved taxpayer dollars and the care of the elderly population of the town. How could he not publish that?

She knew that the nursing home had bought ads, lots of them, and big dollar ones. She understood how the revenue game was played. But from a journalistic standpoint, that was no excuse when the elderly residents were being defrauded. And in fact the entire citizenry was being hoodwinked.

Meghan herself had been forced to write articles that put some of her own friends and acquaintances in a not-so-pleasant light, and some of them had purchased advertising space in this very publication. So there was a double standard when it came to the ones who forked out more than the average business owner

Meghan fought for her story for some time, detailing her reasons for the need to publish the article and even offering to go through and outline every fact in her article, one line at a time if necessary. She also accused him of censorship.

Still, Kingstone, the editor, wanted nothing to do with it and said his decision was final.

Meghan felt defeated, at least for a couple of days. Meghan decided that her efforts were not going to be for nothing but she hadn't figured out how to get the word out to the public.

She felt that she owed it to the residents of the nursing home and she owed it to her friend, Rebecca and her co-workers, who also suffered from low pay and deplorable working conditions. And she owed it to the readers.

She started looking into how to shop her story around. She knew it would be tough because she was a full-time employee of *The Main Informer*. But they weren't buying the story, so she should be able to sell it to someone who was willing to publish it.

Then something happened that completely stunned her. A few days later, the publisher came into her office, shut the door and sat down across from her. He didn't say anything at first. He seemed conflicted. Then suddenly he spoke.

"I've decided to let the story be published, in its entirety," the publisher said.

The words didn't register immediately for Meghan. He continued.

"I've read it over several times and ran it by the paper's lawyer," the publisher said. "He did some fact checking and we came to the conclusion that you are right, about every word in that article. I'm willing to take the lumps if the advertiser pulls out because of it. The government is going to create more problems for him than we will anyway. And you're right, this paper was built on the foundation of integrity and we can't shy away from the ones that make me stay awake late at night. If we're going to be the paper of record, we need to start acting like it."

Meghan wanted to burst into tears of joy. But she restrained herself. She didn't know what to say so mildly uttered, "Thank you."

The publisher talked a little longer but Meghan didn't hear much of it. She was too excited and wanted to get the article placed on the pages of the next edition before he changed his mind.

When he finally finished his monologue, the publisher stood up and reached for the door knob. Then he turned around and said one more thing.

"Oh, by the way, I released Kingstone from his duties as editor today," the publisher said. "He no longer calls the shots around here and has been offered the chance to stay on as a general reporter. I doubt he will, though. You are our new editor, if you want the job.

We'll work out salary and all the details later."

Meghan was even more stunned by this revelation. She didn't know for sure but she was pretty confident that her jaw was on the floor.

CHAPTER 49

Emma Thornton had passed away peacefully in her sleep the night after she confessed everything to her lifelong friend Amelia. Amelia wondered if the spirit of Detective Harrison Parker might have had a hand in avenging his death once Emma finally told the truth.

But nobody even acknowledged or listened to the 105-year-old woman's theory after the night nurse discovered that Emma no longer was breathing during her rounds.

The conclusion was simple: The woman was 100 years old and there really was no need to question the death, or believe that a ghost might have had something to do with it.

CHAPTER 50

Meghan and Rebecca went to the Tirtmansic Cemetery with a bouquet of gardenias and sweet peas, picked from Penelope's school garden, which now blossomed each year at Mercy Angels Nursing Home. The tombstone read: "Amelia Annabelle Adams Spencer; April 12, 1887-April 15, 1993; loving wife, mother and friend to many, mentor and gracious lady."

While Amelia had lived a long, love-filled and fulfilling life, once she learned the truth about what had happened 80 years prior, she lived another six months before finally succumbing to old age.

After a painstaking analysis of the money that was recovered from beneath the cracks in the cobblestone, it was determined that 40 percent of it was Amelia's, 10 percent of it was Emma's by virtue of it being her mother's, although officials distributed it to Amelia because Emma had passed away. The government estimated that the other 50 percent belonged to the taxpayers so kept it as a "finder's fee," thereby allowing the town of Tirtmansic to take in a one-time infusion of revenue. Governmental officials promised to use the funds to improve infrastructure throughout the town and start some tax incentive programs for local, small businesses. They also wanted to improve the rickety cobblestone street that made up Main Street. But the citizens lobbied officials to ensure that while making improvements to the decaying street, they keep the character and charm of a small-town atmosphere that the cobblestones provide. After all, it was a main fixture and reminder of times gone by.

Amelia had willed some of her money to Rebecca and Meghan. While it was not a ton of money, Amelia encouraged the young ladies to pursue their dreams to the fullest extent, whether they had money or not.

The two friends left the cemetery and went to Mug's Pub. Meghan's heel got caught in the cobblestone just outside the bar. They both looked down, looked at each other, shrugged and laughed it off.

Once inside, Rebecca pulled out two ladies' cigars. They also raised their glasses in a toast to honor Amelia Annabelle Adams Spencer, Harrison Parker, his family, and his partner, Lance Cutter. They toasted the four generations of Hendersons and Woodsons, who had carried on the tradition of Mug's Pub. And yes, they even toasted Emma.

Finally, they toasted their newfound friendship.

AFTERWORD FROM THE AUTHOR

The characters, plot, storyline and dialogue in this novel all are fictional, purely figments of my imagination.

However, the buildings that house The Brass Inn/*The Main Informer* and Mug's Pub are based on actual buildings located on Main Street in St. Charles, Missouri. I am drawn to both buildings because I have spent plenty of my adult life inside them.

The building that houses The Brass Inn/*The Main Informer* currently is vacant on one side with Talayna's restaurant on the other. However, from 1989 to 1994, I worked as an assistant sports editor and later sports editor in the building located at 340 N. Main Street when it housed the St. Charles County bureau of the Suburban Journals of Greater St. Louis. I spent a lot of late Friday nights, as late as 4 a.m., alone in the newsroom while others worked upstairs. I also spent a lot of Sunday afternoons completely alone in the building, save for a few stragglers who would come in to work for an hour or two.

Special acknowledgement goes to my brother, Steve, who researched the history of the building for me. According to official records, in the early 1850s, a building was erected at the site and became the American House and later the North Missouri House. Between 1870 and somewhere around 1909, it was called the Galt House Hotel. Records indicate that the Galt House was a first-class hotel known for its hospitality. The building was a hotel and grocery from 1886 until 1909, when it became a hotel and boarding house. Between 1929 and 1947, it was a hotel and several restaurants. It later became home of the *St. Charles Journal.*

When I worked there, the building was in total disrepair, sitting basically alone at the end of North Main Street, on the river side of the street. It also sat directly underneath a crumbling, rotted-out bridge that was almost as creepy during the day as it was at night. We always feared that the bridge would just fall over onto the building. The building's front façade was flat, with just one window that looked out onto a basically vacant portion of Main Street, as that part of the street was blocked off to vehicles during that time frame. The exterior on the front had a faded bluish-grey hue and seemed to just blend into the background, unlike some of the more vibrant buildings that had been restored on south Main Street. Earlier pictures of the building show that there were windows all across the front and side of the second level with larger windows on the first level. Those now have been restored to the original design.

All of us quickly became accustomed to chemicals leaking from above, the stains of who-knows-what on the seemingly centuries-old carpeting, and the dreary atmosphere of plain white, dirty walls. We had no windows except the one in our lunchroom and instead of looking out at the river that flowed–and sometimes flooded literally up to the back door of the building–the newsroom was blocked in with dark brown steel doors that I do not think we could even get open.

While the physical description of the building elicits absolutely no fond memories, it was the people that it housed on a daily basis that gave it charm and character. We literally were a family of reporters, advertising sales reps, front-office staff, bookkeepers and composing specialists who decided to embrace the confines of the building. Most of us probably never appreciated it while we worked there–and in fact always wondered why the fire department did not condemn the building. After thinking about using it as a main setting in my novel for years and working on this project to bring out the best in the building, I have a newfound appreciation of my own, looking beyond just its walls and bland exterior to create a magic that cannot be captured in the physical appearance.

The building that houses Mug's Pub became Rumple's Pub, which is now shuttered as well. My friends and I, known as The Dancing

Girls, began going there after our dance classes held across the street.

Frank Hackney, co-owner of Rumple's, embraced us immediately as his friends and we had endless hours of rip-roaring laughter on Tuesday nights. We later began visiting on packed Friday nights to hear his band, Mid-life Crisis (now called Second Sojourn). Frank gave us the moniker of The Dancing Girls and ultimately is responsible for our friendship. Our love of dance had brought us together but Frank's jokes, laughter, unconditional love and support, and his incredible musical talent solidified our friendship.

Frank knew I was writing this book and that his beloved Rumple's Pub was featured but never had the chance to actually read it because I did not complete it in time. Unfortunately, Frank passed away on June 13, 2010. He may have left this life but his love of life, laughter and music continues in all of our hearts.

***

As for the implied paranormal activity, the experiences described could be fictional or based on true-life experiences.

The nail polish remains one of the most mysterious. One evening, my sister Sharon and I were sitting on my bed talking and suddenly, the bottle of nail polish that I had sitting on my wood nightstand just fell over by itself. It was a bottle with a sturdy rounded base and not easily knocked over, even with the force of a hand. My sister and I stared wide-eyed at each other. We tried to create a sudden gust of air by quickly opening and closing the bedroom door that was right next to the nightstand to see if that might explain it. We also jumped up and down on the floor next to the nightstand and banged on the top of the nightstand with our fists to try to make the bottle fall over, to no avail.

When I worked on my own on those Sunday afternoons or late Friday nights in the Journal building, when people were upstairs in the composing room and I was downstairs in the newsroom, we would hear "unexplained" noises coming from the walls and the basement (where no one dared venture, ever). We even would hear unexplained noises during the day, mixed in with the commotion of the newsroom and advertising office. It could have been critters scampering around the place, or our imaginations running wild while working in a more than 100-year-old building.

Nonetheless, those and some other unexplained experiences with paranormal activity gave me the inspiration to include paranormal activity. Some do not believe ghosts exist. I, for one, believe that at least something exists because I know too many of my own experiences and other people's unexplainable happenings.

ACKNOWLEDGEMENTS

I would like to express my heartfelt gratitude to my family and all of my friends, who have been supportive from the start of this endeavor. I quit my job after nearly 15 years to devote my time to writing the book for a year. Some called it crazy but most called it gutsy, in a good way, I think. They were proud of me for actually doing something with my life instead of just saying that "someday" I would do it. That encouragement alone sustained me through this quest. Special thanks goes to Terry Dean and Diana Stewart, who were the first to read, edit and give me some much-needed and much-appreciated feedback. Thank you also to my lifelong friend, Barb Dunn, who provided me with the guidance of her legal expertise to make this happen.

As I wrote, I had two faithful Boston Terrier companions—Mulligan and Madison—at my side. They were content to snooze while I created, and only bossed me around when they wanted massages or wanted to go out and be fed.

A special note of gratitude for my parents, Ronald and Earlyne, who gave me a solid childhood and the foundation to achieve anything. They always encouraged my sister, brother and me to develop our interests and they helped us foster our talents, never standing in the way of our desire to accomplish something. They taught all of us about perseverance, determination, dedication and devotion but mostly, they taught us about love, respect and compassion. I know how proud they would be that I actually took the risk and did something that I wanted to do with my life. My only regret is that both were taken from us far too soon and that neither one of them is here to read the final product.

I thank my older sister, Sharon, who is more of a numbers person but understands my devotion to the written word. When we were younger, as my older sister, she always encouraged me in everything that I did. When I told her of my plan to write this book, she never hesitated in her encouragement and support to just go for it. I also thank my baby brother, Steve, who is a talented writer and understands the struggles I had in finally putting the thoughts in my head down on paper. Steve had been pushing me for years to take the leap of faith and write my book. He has served as my personal sounding board when I struggled on language or plot or character development, or just to sit down and actually write.

This book is dedicated first and foremost to my family, because without their love, support and faith in me, this could have never come to fruition. It also is dedicated to my friends, who are part of my family and enrich my life for always being there for me. I am not going to name names as there are too many people to acknowledge and I fear I would inadvertently leave someone out. But they know who they are and I hope they know how much I cherish their friendships. My family and friends are the people who have supported me throughout all of the trials, tribulations and great joys of my life. Without all of them, I could have not accomplished this great adventure into the unknown.

BOOK CLUB DISCUSSION POINTS

Cracks in the Cobblestone is a mystery that includes messages about taking risks, fiscal responsibility, journalistic integrity, love and forgiveness, the power of friendship and compassion, tapping into knowledge and education as a guiding force, and whether a spiritual or paranormal power really can influence our actions.

1. What risks have you taken in your personal and professional lives? What kind of impact did those decisions have on your life and overall well-being?

2. Are you fiscally responsible? Is your government? Your employer? What are realistic approaches to being fiscally responsible while still providing a high level of quality in services delivered? What steps have you had to take to become more fiscally responsible and what should our local, state and federal governments do to achieve that goal?

3. Identify media organizations (print, television, radio, blogs, etc.) and individuals that you feel do not have journalistic integrity and explain why you feel that way. Now identify organizations and individuals who exemplify a dedication to upholding journalistic ethics and integrity, and explain why.

4. Describe the people you love and why. Identify what behaviors and actions you would be willing to forgive or not forgive for each one and explain why.

5. Describe the people who have been your closest friends, how you met and why you believe you have remained friends. What im-

pact have they had on your life and your decisions? Why do you acknowledge and honor their opinions over others?

6. What kind of education and knowledge have you developed over the years? Was it through classroom education, training and seminars, reading books on your own, other people's influences, monitoring current events? How has your educational background prepared you to deal with your job, your life and the people you interact with on a daily basis?

7. As for the spirits, ghosts or paranormal activity - I intentionally did not designate the "spirits" in this story as ghosts. Some people believe in ghosts, others do not. Some people believe in some kind of unseen force that can influence us. Some believe that after our loved ones depart, their souls remain and guide us while others believe that the spirit is gone when the physical is gone. What do you believe? Do ghosts exist? Are there spirits lingering around us? Is it just in our imaginations? Do ghosts or spirits linger because of unresolved issues before they can move on? Can we really interact with ghosts and spirits to forge change or resolution, even if we never met the physical being that now is in spiritual form? Does it just make us feel better to believe that our loved ones still exist in some unknown manner after their physical existence ceases?

ABOUT THE AUTHOR

Susan E. Sagarra, a native of St. Louis, Mo., is a consultant in writing, editing and public/media relations. She previously was the inaugural managing editor of a St. Louis-based newspaper, *West Newsmagazine,* for nearly 15 years and most recently was editor of the Show-Me Institute. Sagarra has worked as the first communications director of the Gateway Section of the PGA; a sports editor for the Suburban Journals of Greater St. Louis (St. Charles County bureau); and a public relations intern for the St. Louis Cardinals baseball team.

Sagarra has earned numerous journalism awards, including first place in the National Federation of Press Women-Missouri Chapter annual contest. She also received the Missouri Women Legislators' Award for her coverage of Missouri state government.

Sagarra received a bachelor of arts degree in English and communications from Lindenwood College and a master of arts degree in communications from Lindenwood.

Her passions include dancing, reading, writing, cooking, listening to music, watching movies and St. Louis Cardinals baseball, relaxing on the beach, and spending time with family, friends and her dogs.

Made in the USA
Charleston, SC
25 October 2015